DARE TO TEMPT

Dare Nation Novel #2

NEW YORK TIMES BESTSELLING AUTHOR

Carly Phillips

DARE TO TEMPT

**He's a smooth talking jock in trouble
She's the solution to his problems.
Love is the last thing they expected to find.**

Damon Prescott had it all. Star quarterback. Money. Fame. Now? He's being accused of taking performance enhancing drugs and banned from the sport and team he loves.

Determined to prove he's innocent, he hires tough as nails private investigator, Evie Wolfe. She's able to bring a man to his knees with a glare, yet sensual in ways that take him off guard—and she's everything Damon didn't know he needed.

Evie's used to men dismissing her, especially playboys like Damon Prescott so she's not buying the sexual lines he's trying to sell. She's with him to do a job, nothing more. But you know what they say about the best laid plans? Sometimes you end up between the sheets with an arrogant football player anyway.

But when the case is over, can Damon convince Evie she's the only woman for him or will she leave him tied up in love?

A stand-alone novel

Chapter One

Damon Prescott's life had gone from golden to shit in an instant. Or rather in one violent football play gone wrong. He refused to watch the reviews of his injury. The slam of his head against the turf and the shattering pain before he blacked out were vivid enough in his mind.

Another concussion should have been the worst of his problems. Instead he'd also tested positive for performance-enhancing drugs in a random test and had been suspended immediately. As if he'd touch the stuff. No unknown supplements went into his body. Period. So how the fuck had he tested positive not just once but on a second check as well?

A knock sounded at his door and he pushed himself up from his couch, his head still pounding a week later. Even his ears continued to ring. He walked slowly to the front entrance, opened up, and let his family into his home. It was the second meeting since the results had come back.

The people entering his house weren't just family, they were his team. That team included Dare Nation, a sports management firm his brother Austin owned along with their uncle Paul Dare.

Austin, his oldest sibling and his agent, strode in first, his executive assistant and girlfriend, Quinn Stone, by his side. Austin patted him on the back. Quinn smiled and murmured her apologies for what was going on.

Next came Bri, his sister and publicist. "Don't worry, I've got you covered," she promised him, pulling him into a hug.

He'd deliberately kept this gathering tight. He didn't want his mother, Christine, here. She was already upset by the situation and his injury. His brother Jaxon was at baseball practice and couldn't be here. And Braden was abroad with Doctors Without Borders. Paul was at the office, fending off the press and holding down the fort.

But they did need a plan. First of all, the season started in two weeks, and Damon didn't want to miss being allowed on the field for the first four games due to a suspension. He was appealing and should hear soon what the verdict was.

Austin cleared his throat. "Let me start by saying everyone in this room knows you didn't cheat. But we also know the likelihood of winning on appeal in this zero-tolerance era and it's not good."

Damon clenched his fists at his sides. "I did not

take a banned substance."

His brother stared at him, his expression somber. "Players are responsible for what is in their bodies and a positive test will not be excused because a player was unaware he was taking a prohibited substance." He repeated the words from the players' collective bargaining agreement.

Words Damon already knew by heart.

"Golden Tate was taking fertility treatments he didn't know contained prohibited substances," Austin continued. "And if that doesn't tug on the committee's heartstrings, I don't know what will."

"Tate self-reported before he tested positive and they still didn't cut him any slack," Bri said.

Despite the fact that Damon heard his siblings, he refused to give up without a fight, and believing in himself was priority one. "I still say we go forward as if we'll win. We thought we'd hear by now. Maybe it's a good sign they're taking their time."

His brother and sister glanced at each other and nodded.

"We figured you'd say as much," Bri said. "So, I've got an idea. Well, thanks to Quinn, I have an idea."

Damon grinned. "You're the family fixer. Of course you do." But he rubbed his chest, which grew tight any time he let himself think about the mess he was in.

Without admitting it to his siblings, even he knew that the only out given on appeal was when the testing had been compromised. He couldn't prove his had. But he refused to give up until forced to.

He was one of the team captains despite his young age, and it was a contract year, for fuck's sake. The positive test gave Ian Dare, his team owner, every reason not to offer him the deal he deserved as the up-and-coming star quarterback of the Miami Thunder.

"You've spoken to Ray Benson's PI?" Damon asked of the lawyer Dare Nation used and Austin himself had used when his baby girl had been left on his doorstep.

So much had changed in such a short time.

Bri shook her head. "Nope. I have someone better. A licensed PI whose work I value." She clasped her hand behind her back and rocked on her heels, grinning in a way Damon didn't trust.

His gut churned and he glanced at Austin. "You wouldn't let her fuck me over, right?"

Austin rolled his eyes. "We're all on your side. Though I will say Bri's plan is a little … unorthodox."

Before either could elaborate, the doorbell rang. Damon raised his eyebrows. "Who is that?"

"I've got it," Bri said and rushed to the front of the house to let the unknown visitor in.

Damon waited, and seconds later, Bri strode back

into the room with his biggest nightmare by her side. Evie Wolfe, Quinn's best friend, a *licensed PI*, and a woman Damon hadn't been able to get out of his head since the day they'd met, walked in.

Evie wasn't anything like the typical female he was used to. No red-soled stilettos or designer handbags for her. A pair of scuffed leather boots and ripped jeans that fit her like a glove, along with a black leather jacket she rarely removed, were her normal attire. And damned if it wasn't sexy.

"Hi, Damon." She eyed him with an amused grin.

"Evie."

They'd met the first time at Dare Nation. She'd come off an all-night watch and strode in to meet Quinn for lunch wearing a similar outfit, jeans that hugged her ass, a long-sleeve tight top that showed off her full breasts and ample cleavage, her face makeup free and her mouth sassy.

Damon had been sitting outside Austin's office while he was on a phone call, taken one look at the woman with the gorgeous dark hair hanging loose around her shoulders, not his usual type, yet he'd been drooling. Not literally.

"Staring at something?" she'd asked him with snark.

He'd held up his hands. "Just admiring the view."

Austin had walked out of his office at that moment

and smacked him in the head with the papers in his hand. From that day on, they'd gotten under each other's skin. He didn't know what it was about her, but he was more comfortable across the room and not close enough to smell her musky perfume.

"Well, who wants to hear the plan?" Bri asked.

He folded his hands across his chest and glared at his sister, who was enjoying her moment way too much. "Go on."

"You tested positive for PEDs and you think you were set up," Evie said.

"I know I was set up," he said through clenched teeth.

Evie nodded. "And you need to know who did it, how, and why."

"Which is why I need a private investigator."

She grinned. "One who can stay by your side and get into places a regular PI can't. Places a girlfriend can go." She sidled up to him, rubbing her leather-clad arm against his bare one, and damned if his body didn't respond, his cock perking up.

Then her words registered. "Oh, hell no." He didn't *date* women, for real or pretend.

He fucked them and sent them on their way. And he didn't think he had a shot in hell of anyone believing he was together with Evie and her leather-clad body. Despite what his dick wanted, something he'd yet to understand.

"Damon, think about it. You need someone who can evaluate the people in your life."

"In case you forgot, the suspension means I can't do much with anyone on the team," he reminded her.

"Yes, but they can't stop you from *running into someone* in a public place." She put quotation marks around the words she'd emphasized. "So, if there's anyone you want to meet, he can subtly arrange it. This is exactly what we wanted," Bri said with excitement in her voice. "And most importantly, I trust her."

Evie checked him with her hip. "Come on. How can it hurt? Unless you're afraid of me?"

He gritted his teeth. "Of course I'm not afraid of you. I just don't think we're ... compatible or that it'll look real," he said, scanning from her scuffed boots to her windblown hair, ignoring the fact that he thought she was gorgeous in an understated and quite unique way.

She stepped in front of him and braced her hands on her hips. A flush of red stained her cheeks.

"Embarrassed to be seen with me?" she asked, telling him he'd been right. He'd hit a nerve. "Because I promise you I can dress up and play a role as well as any one of those cleat chasers you and your buddies hang out with," she assured him.

From across the room, Austin glared. Because Evie was Quinn's best friend? Or because Damon was being stubborn about a plan Austin had faith in? Probably a combination of both.

"Tell you what," Austin said. "Let's go to Allstars tonight and test the theory of you two as a couple."

Damon considered the idea. The upscale bar would have enough people there to see them together and for them to get a feel for whether people familiar with Damon bought the concept of Evie as his girlfriend. He could handle testing things out. "Fine."

"Don't sound so thrilled." Evie scowled at him. "I'm going home. Apparently it's going to take me a long time to pull myself together for His Highness over here." She jerked a thumb his way, making Damon feel like shit.

He hadn't meant to insult her, just explain why he didn't believe this plan would work.

"I'm going with you." Quinn picked up her purse, shot a nasty look at Damon, and followed her best friend out, leaving Damon with his siblings. And he damn well knew if Quinn was pissed at him, Austin was, too.

"Well, that went well," he said aloud.

"Because you're an asshole," Bri said. "Evie didn't deserve to be insulted, considering she was willing to help you."

Damon stiffened his shoulders. "I didn't think I was offending her. Just being honest."

"You as much as told her people wouldn't think she was your type, bro." Austin leaned against the wall unit in the family room.

"Actually, the way he looked her over all but insinuated she wasn't feminine enough," Bri said.

He winced.

"Okay, look, you're not in a position to fight this," Bri reminded him. "A regular PI can't talk to the people around you. She can. So suck it up and make nice."

"I'll see you tonight. I'll text you the time. Want us to pick you up? You shouldn't drive if you're still having symptoms," Austin said.

"I'll take a driver." He had a feeling Quinn would lay into him if they were alone. And the three of them might show up with Evie.

Damon needed time to prepare himself for the acting job of a lifetime.

"I'll see you tonight. I expect you to be on your best behavior," Austin said.

Damon frowned. "Are you speaking as my brother or my agent?"

"Both." Austin stood up straight and started for the door. "And you could start with an apology to Evie."

Bri smirked, liking when someone else was getting called on the carpet. "Hang in there, Damon. You can trust Evie to get the job done." She paused. "As long as you're not an asshole to her, that is."

Ignoring her comment, he let his family out and leaned against the door with a groan. He was exhausted and needed to lie down if he was going to go out for an hour or so tonight. At least Allstars was quiet, known for letting athletes and famous people mingle in peace without groupies begging for autographs or signed boobs.

Speaking of boobs, he wondered how much cleavage Evie would show. Jesus, he was an asshole. Blaming the concussion, he headed upstairs to take a nap before his performance later tonight.

*   *   *

Evie yanked a hairbrush through her long hair, knotted from the ride in her convertible. She stood in front of the mirror on the wall in her bedroom, trying to get the tangles out while she was thinking about Damon.

"Stupid jackass," Evie muttered. "Brainless, no-good, dark-haired, sexy, tattooed, bastard with full lips, tanned skin, and indigo-blue eyes." She blew out a puff of air and ignored the tingling of her skin and the rush of arousal that always accompanied her thinking about Damon Prescott.

Quinn sat cross-legged on the bed and Evie could see her in the reflection. "He didn't mean to be a jackass. He's in pain and he's frustrated."

Evie turned to her best friend. "Are you standing up for him?"

"No." She held up her hands, making it clear whose side she was on. "I just don't want you to lose out on a good job." She didn't want to lose it, either.

Six months ago, she'd left her job as an investigator at the Miami District Attorney's Office for reasons she didn't like to think about and had gone into business for herself. Proving Damon Prescott innocent would boost her business, and as a new PI, she needed a high-profile client.

"Not to mention we need you," Quinn went on. "Ignore Damon's attitude. I'm sure Austin straightened him out when we left."

"Fine but if he says anything rude tonight, he's getting a stiletto in his foot."

Quinn grinned, a genuine smile. Since falling in love with Austin and taking on the role of mom to the baby girl he'd found on his doorstep, she was lighter and happier than she'd ever been.

"Or we could sic your cop dad and all four of your brothers on him. That could be fun. If he wasn't injured, that is."

Evie rolled her eyes. "Now that you're attached to

the family, you're no fun," Evie said. "You're too nice."

"What are you going to wear tonight?" Quinn ignored her comment, slid off the bed, and headed to her closet to look through her dresses.

Evie narrowed her gaze, remembering how that handsome jerk had looked her over and found her lacking. Damon Prescott pushed all her wrong buttons. From the day she'd been introduced to him at Dare Nation, he'd treated her like an annoyance. She couldn't deny the idea of dressing up and seeing his jaw drop at the sight of her held a lot of appeal.

"This." She joined Quinn by her walk-in and reached for the black one-armed dress that draped her body and hit mid-thigh.

"Oooh, pretty. Reminds me of my red gown, and Austin nearly ripped that right off me." She grinned at an obvious memory Evie didn't want to know about.

"Keep the dirty details to yourself."

"You know … you don't need to cover your arm. The scar has healed and—"

"We don't discuss it, remember?" Evie laid the dress out on the bed and smoothed her hand over the soft fabric.

"*You* don't discuss it. I do because the past doesn't define who you are, no matter what you think." Quinn put her hands on her hips and faced Evie. "Now I'd love to lend you a gold dress that would look gorgeous with your skin tone. It drapes down the back and both arms are bare." She went back to the subject at hand.

Evie shook her head. "A married woman hired me to catch her husband cheating and it turned out he was my fiancé. A man I hadn't pegged as dangerous and I should have. I'd say that shows a decided lack in judgment on my part when I prided myself on being a smart chick." And that was just one of the reasons she'd left her job. She couldn't face people giving her that sympathetic look or questioning her skills because she hadn't seen what was right in front of her.

"You're still a smart chick. John was a slick bastard. He conned his wife as well as you and she's an investment banker. I don't think she's stupid. Do you? What about the other women who've been duped by pathetic men? Who's at fault?"

"I hear you, but it isn't the same thing. I need my instincts, and if I can't trust those, then I have issues I need to work through. And *this* is a reminder of my mistakes." She held out her arm with the angry red scar running along her forearm.

"I don't want it exposed for me to see every day or be asked about it and have to explain the knife wound." Because John, once he'd been caught, had been so angry, he hadn't hesitated to hurt her.

Tears formed in Quinn's eyes and she pulled Evie

into a hug, something she still wasn't used to, even though Quinn had always been a hugger. Her brothers were more the shoulder-slapping types unless they were scared for her well-being, but they always had her back. Always. And they'd have gone after John if she hadn't insisted she didn't want them to end up behind bars.

"Okay, fine. I'm not going to give up trying to convince you that you're the strong, kick-ass woman you always were, but wear that dress. When he gets a look at you, Damon is going to swallow his tongue. Now let's see the shoes."

A couple of hours later, Quinn had gone home to see Austin and Jenny, her adorable little baby, and change for tonight.

Evie stood in front of the mirror once more and she didn't recognize herself. It had been a long time since she'd dressed up for any reason or gone all out for any occasion.

She'd put self-tanner on her legs, arms, chest, and face, because she never had the time to relax and lie in the sun. Her face was completely made up, including wearing false eyelashes, her lips were plump, and her brown eyes wide.

The dress accentuated her curves while the designer red-soled heels hurt her damned feet. Though she had to admit she liked the Chanel purse she owned for times when she had to look a certain way. And to-night? She appeared every inch the pro football player's girlfriend. Damon Prescott wasn't going to know what hit him.

* * *

Given his concussion symptoms, Damon couldn't drink alcohol. It was hard enough to hold up his head, but he understood the need to be at the bar. If he wanted to discover who had set him up, he had to put a plan in motion, and testing Evie and their chemistry was a start.

He occupied a table at Allstars. On one side of Damon, Austin and Quinn were cuddled close together. Bri sat next to her friend Macy Walker, and beside her was Damon's brother Jaxon, who never missed a chance to go out and party, even if the night was a mellow one.

Behind them but at a nearby table, close enough to share conversation if they wanted to, were other guys from his team, Devon White, his running back, and James Slater, his wide receiver.

Marnie, the cocktail waitress, an auburn-haired, stunning woman, knew most of them by name and took drink orders, fawning over Damon and his injury.

Beside him, Austin shifted in his seat so many times Damon grew agitated. "Bro, what the fuck?

You're annoying as hell." Damon elbowed Austin in the arm.

Quinn grinned. "Your brother took Marnie home the night he found Jenny on his doorstep."

Damon tipped his neck back and burst out laughing, immediately regretting the motion when his head began to pound. "I have to admit that was worth the pain."

Austin shot him a dirty look, but Quinn merely cuddled up closer to Austin and continued to smile.

"At least you're not the jealous type," Damon said to the pretty woman with dark hair and green eyes, who seemed custom-made for Austin.

Not that they hadn't had their issues. Between Quinn not wanting kids, Austin being handed a baby by another woman, and Quinn being his brother's assistant, they'd overcome a lot in a short time.

"That's only because Marnie's keeping her distance from your brother." Quinn's gaze traveled across the room to where Marnie filled drinks by the bar.

"And that's because you're wrapped around me, staking your claim. Besides, I only have eyes for you." Austin leaned over and pressed a kiss against her lips.

"You two are making me want to barf." Bri picked up her bottle of Blue Moon and took a long sip.

"Amen." Jaxon lifted his drink in agreement.

Macy, an attractive woman with long blonde hair,

followed suit.

"So Macy, you feel the same way? No commitment for you?" Jaxon asked, his eyes glittering with interest in the attractive woman who was their sister's good friend.

She shook her head. "I'd never have the time."

Jaxon nudged her arm. "There's always time for fun."

"Says the man who helps keep social media active?" She fluttered her lashes at him and refocused on Bri. Obviously, she had Jaxon pegged.

And his brother, not used to being dismissed, frowned, causing Damon to chuckle.

Jaxon shot him the finger and Damon laughed harder. Macy had moxie and he liked her. Bri and Macy had met recently at an exercise class and become friends. From the little Damon knew, Macy had her hands full with the stepsister she was raising. Her life was complicated and Bri tried to get Macy out to have fun whenever she could. And if she knocked Jaxon down a peg, even better.

Damon turned from his amusement for the night and glanced at the entrance to the bar. A couple stood at the hostess stand, where they were led to an empty table. He watched them be seated, waiting for Evie, growing annoyed that she couldn't make it on time like everyone else.

From behind him, James let out a low whistle. "Now *she's* fucking hot."

Damon turned to look. A brunette, her hair hanging in long, spiral curls, stood at the hostess stand, looking down. A short black dress with one sleeve clung to a rocking body. Her legs were long, her heels high, and if his head weren't still throbbing, he could imagine them wrapped around his waist as he pounded into her, hard and deep.

She lifted her head and immediately met his gaze. He found himself looking at a bombshell with pouty bright red lips, cat-like liner around her brown eyes, and a knowing smirk on that familiar mouth. "Holy shit."

"I think this is what they call Damon eating his words," Austin said, sounding amused.

"You didn't think she could do it, did you?" Quinn met his gaze, judgment in her expression, and she was right.

"No, I did not."

Before he could say more, Evie sashayed across the room, every male eye on her as she strode directly toward him. Her stare locked on his, she stopped in front of him.

"Hi, honey. Sorry I'm late." And with that pronouncement, she sat down *in his lap*, wrapped her arms around his neck, and settled her mouth against his.

He stiffened in surprise and she slid her tongue over his bottom lip, causing his cock to rise and his mouth to part. Next thing he knew, he'd gripped her neck, pulled her tight against him, and was kissing the hell out of her in public.

Damon had made out with many females, but he'd never wanted to get lost inside a woman the way he did with Evie. Evie. Jesus. Sanity threatened to return, but she ran her fingers through his hair and he forgot he'd been about to pull back. He slid his tongue over her lips and speared inside once more.

A whistle broke the moment, and Damon jerked his head back, taking the pain as his due. What had he been thinking, devouring Evie in a place he frequented? It was one thing to test the theory of them being plausible as a couple, another to stake a claim on her.

"You didn't tell us you had yourself a hot woman," James said. "Keeping her to yourself?"

Damon drew in a calming breath. His dick wasn't cooperating and he was certain Evie felt it against her thigh, but he needed to sell *them* and now was the beginning.

"We were keeping our relationship quiet, but after Damon's injury, we decided life's short, why hide our feelings?" Evie spoke before Damon could jump in with an explanation. "Right, honey bear?"

He caught himself before he glared her way. He

cupped his hand on her thigh. "Right, snookums."

From beside him, he heard his siblings stifling laughter. But he had to admit, he'd underestimated Evie Wolfe. She could definitely pass as an NFL player's girlfriend and he didn't mind having her acting as his.

"Okay, let's discuss things," Austin said in a low voice. "Now that we know you two can act as a couple, Evie, what's your plan?"

"I'd like to talk to my *boyfriend* alone and in private. Get a recounting of what happened, find out who he thinks could have it in for him on the team." She shifted on his lap, leaning back to look into his eyes, and though he didn't know if her thigh movement was deliberate, his body liked the feeling of her rubbing against his cock.

He cleared his throat. "Why don't you come by my house tomorrow morning and we can discuss things."

She nodded. "That works."

Austin stared at them, taking in her arm wrapped around his neck. "You two also need to learn about each other and get your stories straight on how you met, how long you've been together under the radar, things like that."

They both nodded.

As the family dispersed, Damon met Evie's gaze. "I think you can get your own seat now. Or even better, it's time to go home. I don't think my head can take much more. I need to lie down."

Concern etched her pretty features. "I didn't realize you were still in pain. You didn't drive here, did you?"

He knew better than to shake his head. "No. I took a service."

"I'll bring you home. My car's a little small but you can squeeze in."

He noted she remained on his lap, her thighs on his still-hard cock. "That's okay. I don't want you to go out of your way."

She tilted her head, causing those gorgeous curls to spiral over her shoulder. "And leave my boyfriend to go home alone? Nope. Let's hit the road, honey bear."

Finally, she stood up, but that left him in an awkwardly *hard* situation.

*   *   *

After Evie dropped him off, Damon climbed into bed, nude, as usual. He lay back against the pillows, remembering the moment he'd realized the gorgeous woman at the hostess stand was Evie.

She affected him, the tough PI and the soft woman who'd sat on his lap. What a mix of contradictions she'd turned out to be. He thought he'd noticed her due to her alluring features, but Evie was more than a good-looking woman. Apart from the fact that she also rocked a dress like a goddess, she was not just smart but intelligent.

And she kissed like a fucking dream. Just the thought of her mouth on his, her thighs on his lap, and his cock thickened at the memory of how badly he'd wanted to thrust up and have more than just a pretend moment in time. He could even imagine it. Her eager and willing in his arms, tasting like the sweetest treat, her swiveling hips nearly causing him to come in his pants.

As he thought of Evie, he gripped his dick and began to work his palm up and down his shaft. But unlike in the past, he had a face to the woman holding him in her hand. Eyes closed, he envisioned it was Evie's palm and not his own, *her* grip tight, pre-come helping to lubricate as he slid up and down.

He thought about her dark hair draping across his chest, her full lips, mouth parting to suck him in deep until he hit the back of her throat, and it didn't take long. Suddenly he was coming hard, spurting over his abdomen and hand.

He blew out a long breath and groaned, wondering how long his palm was going to be a substitute for the real thing. He cleaned up and went to sleep, the woman he couldn't forget on his mind.

Chapter Two

The following morning, Evie arrived at Damon's house ready to talk to him, gain an understanding of his situation, and discover how he'd reached the point of testing positive for PEDs. She wanted lists of his friends, enemies, anyone jealous of him, and anyone he'd interacted with over the last month.

She hadn't been able to chat with him last night. He'd fallen asleep in the car on the way home, his knees squished up to his chest in her front seat. And she was definitely as concerned about his injury as she was about his test results. She'd driven, occasionally catching a glimpse of him as he dozed. His superstar arrogance, his expensive clothing, and the gorgeous, chiseled face contrasted with her down-to-earth way of looking at the world and her basic clothes from Target. Not that she'd worn them today.

Knowing his situation made him a magnet for paparazzi, she dressed up in case she was photographed coming or going from his house. There were cars lined up the street, and she was certain paps with long-range lenses were inside, making her glad she'd thought ahead and looked the part of a woman a man like Damon Prescott would date.

In the real world, they couldn't be more different, but she was drawn to Damon anyway. Not for one minute did she believe he'd cheated in the sport he loved. And that was one of the most appealing things about him, his dedication to his career. Okay, there were also his soft lips that knew how to devour her mouth like the professional player he was.

The kiss meant for show had turned into something that felt real. His tongue delving between her lips and tangling with hers, her nipples pebbling beneath her dress, and the moisture in her thong had all been genuine. So had the thick erection she'd felt pressed against her thigh. She pushed those unwanted thoughts away because, attraction aside, they were like oil and water. And he had no desire to be with a woman like her.

He'd made that perfectly clear when the idea of her playing his girlfriend had come up, which was why she'd gotten a definite jolt of satisfaction at the look on his face when she'd walked into Allstars last night. His gaze had darkened, that gorgeous stare settling on her lips, and she'd never felt more feminine and powerful. But at the end of the day, she was who she was, a woman who liked casual clothing and speaking her mind, and she didn't want to care whether a pro football player found her lacking in any way.

She rang his doorbell and, when he didn't answer, hit the button again. His house was located in an exclusive Miami neighborhood, a huge structure with gorgeous colored shrubbery, trees, and flowers surrounding the white stucco set back from the road. A gate surrounded the perimeter of the house, open at the drive. And neighbors were far apart, further proof that the cars did indeed hold paparazzi looking for the million-dollar photograph.

She rang again, growing concerned.

She was about to knock once more when the door opened and a sexy, disheveled Damon stood before her. He wore a pair of low-riding gray sweatpants that revealed more than they covered, and her stare lingered on the bulge in his pants and the deep V on the sides of his hips.

He cleared his throat.

Caught, she forced her gaze up past his tanned chest to meet his amused expression, heat rising to her face. But as he took in her carefully made-up face and chosen outfit, his indigo eyes darkened with definite approval, making her glad she'd chosen the white low V-neck lace camisole tank that revealed a good amount of cleavage, her beloved leather jacket that covered her scar, a pair of tight designer jeans, and a pair of high wedge shoes that showed off her coral-colored toenails.

He met her stare and grinned.

She forced a smile at the damned good-looking man. His hair appeared as if he'd run his hand through it … or had just gotten out of bed, and she wished she'd been there with him. The errant thought rushed through her and she stifled a groan. She was here for business. Even if that kiss last night and that hot body now had rocked her world.

"Did I wake you?" she asked, hoping she sounded composed.

"It's fine. I just need some coffee." He turned and walked away, apparently expecting her to follow him.

"I take it you're not a morning person," she said to herself and shut the door.

She found him in the kitchen with a K-cup in hand. "Want one?" he asked before popping it into the machine.

"No, thank you." She'd had her caffeine earlier at home. "Are you up to talking?" she asked.

"Yeah. Just dealing with the remnants of this head injury. It's annoying as fuck. I'm not used to the constant spinning, throbbing, and general dizziness. And if I win the appeal, they're not going to let me play until I can pass concussion protocol."

"I've read up on that." She nodded understanding-ly.

He gestured for her to take a seat at the table, and she chose a chair and lowered herself into it.

His coffee finished dripping into a large mug, and he sat down, obviously taking it black. "So, what do you want to know?" he asked as he took a sip.

She pulled a notepad from her purse, foregoing her phone app or taping. "I want your daily schedule, what you do, who you see, what supplements, if any, you take, things like that. Who likes you, who's jealous of you, who tolerates you? And after we discuss your weekdays and friends, I want to know your weekend schedule for the last month including the women you've been with. So, take out your calendar and get to it."

"That's pretty thorough," he said, sounding impressed.

She nodded. "It's going to help us figure out who's setting you up."

He placed the mug on the table, picked up his phone, and leaned back in his chair, scrolling through his apps, she assumed.

"Okay, on a normal day, when I'm not suspended, I wake up around five a.m., drink a smoothie—"

"Where do you get the protein powder?" she asked.

"From my trainer, recommended by him and my backup quarterback. When I'm at the stadium, the puppy dog brings me one every morning."

She jerked her head up at the nickname. "Puppy dog?"

Damon smirked. "Gregory Emerson's a lick-my-balls—" He cleared his throat. "I mean a lick-my-ass kind of kid. Not great at throwing the ball, which is an issue, but he wouldn't hurt me."

She narrowed her gaze, not as sure as he was, and wrote down the name on her notepad. "Go on. What's next on your schedule?"

"I get dressed, head to the gym at the stadium. I work out with Jimmy O'Roarke, the head trainer."

She added to the list. "Who else do you train with?"

For the next thirty minutes, she wrote down the names of other team trainers, doctors, and players who were usually around at the same time as him. Knowing they'd revisit each person, she let him talk.

"How about jealousy? Anyone you have issues with?"

He treated her to his most winning smile. "Every-one loves me."

She frowned despite being drawn to that grin. "Be serious."

He sobered, his expression somber. "I'm damned serious. I don't know anyone who dislikes me enough to sabotage my entire career." He put his mug down and shoved it away.

She felt bad for him and understood how much was on the line. "Okay, who would benefit with you out? Any other player?" she asked.

He drummed his fingers on the table, then met her gaze. "No."

"Let's move on to women. The paparazzi like photographing you with the various females on your arm. Did you dump any of them and piss them off?" She'd already done a quick internet search and knew he wasn't the long-term dating type.

"I hate to sound like a cliché but they know the deal before we go out. I'm not interested in a relationship."

She wondered why he didn't want romantic entanglements, but it wasn't part of her job description to ask. "I'd still like the names of the most recent women you've been with."

He rambled them off, then braced his hands on the table and stood. "And I'm finished for the day. There's not enough coffee for this shit."

He rose, walking to the counter and putting his coffee cup in the sink.

She gathered her things and rose to her feet. She'd peppered him with enough questions and had sufficient information to begin digging into the people he surrounded himself with. "I'll let you get back to your day and I'll be in touch."

"Sounds good." He turned, folding his arms across that golden muscular chest. "Thank you, Evie," he said gruffly.

She nodded, understanding the depth of meaning behind the words. "I'll work as quickly as I can. I know the appeal is going to come down fast."

"Yeah. It is." His tone told her which way he thought the decision would go.

A few steps ahead of her, he walked her to the entryway and opened the door, when she saw what looked like dark marks on the upper part of his back and shoulder.

"What's this?" she asked, coming up behind him and touching his skin, her body immediately reacting to his heat and masculine scent. "It looks like adhesive," she said, her voice husky. She rubbed at the marks, and some residue came off on the pads of her fingers.

"Probably remnants from the pain patch my trainer gave me. Now that I'm suspended, he said he'd meet me at his private office, not at the stadium," he said, his upper torso shuddering at her touch.

He turned slowly, placing one hand on the doorframe, blocking her in with his body, her nipples puckering at his warmth and closeness.

"If you didn't notice last night, you affect me,

Evie. A lot. And if you keep touching me, I'm going to want to taste you again. So, if you want to have any hope of keeping this a purely professional, fake relationship, step back."

She swallowed hard, her mouth going dry at his sexually honest words, and she did as he suggested. She stepped back.

"Umm … what are the chances you still have the patch?" she asked, her voice raspy as she brought them back to business. "I'd like to have it tested. See if there's anything in the medication that shouldn't be."

Surprise flickered in his expression. "As a matter of fact, it's in the garbage upstairs. Hang on and I'll be right back."

He headed upstairs and she leaned against the doorframe he'd used earlier, closed her eyes, and groaned. She'd thought this assignment would be easy. Help Damon find out who'd targeted him and set him up. Sure, she knew she was attracted to him, but she'd never thought the feeling was mutual.

There was a part of her that resented the fact that he liked this Evie, the one who dressed for a part, not the woman she was beneath the makeup, spiral hair, and heels. Another part of her reminded herself it didn't matter which Evie he liked because he didn't do relationships and she'd sworn off men.

Knowing how badly her judgment sucked with the

opposite sex, she knew better than to let herself fall for the playboy who'd already made his lack of intentions with any woman clear.

*   *   *

After Evie left, he didn't have much to do. He couldn't work out, not with the way his head felt. Instead he decided to sit outside and get some sun. He changed into a pair of shorts and headed out back. He settled on one of the recliner chairs in his fenced-in yard, free from paparazzi unless they were hanging from the trees above, and let out a groan.

Trying to relax when his world was in upheaval wasn't easy, but he managed to do some deep breathing exercises he'd learned and calmed down, dozing beneath the hot sun.

The sound of his cell ringing woke him, and he grabbed for the phone, unsure how much time had passed. "Yeah. Hello." He answered without checking the screen because the sun's glare prevented him from seeing who was calling.

"Hello?"

"Damon!" Bri's voice sounded in his ear. "Have you seen social media?"

"No. Been napping and I can't see out here. I'll go inside. What's going on?" He swung his legs over the side of the lounge.

"You and Evie went viral. There's a pic on TNZ's Instagram of you two in the doorway of your house this morning. *Who's the woman seen leaving Damon Prescott's house early this morning after a hot night?*" Bri asked in a faux-journalistic type voice.

"What the hell? She came over this morning to talk. She didn't stay over last night."

"Well, guess what? Better they be speculating about your love life than whether you used PEDs. And that picture? Evie's hands all over your bare back? Whew." He could imagine her waving her hand in front of her face. "There'll be no doubt in anyone's mind what's going on between the two of you." Bri sounded downright gleeful.

He didn't mind that the press had picked up on his fake relationship with Evie. That had been the point. He just hadn't been paying attention to the cars outside his house and he should have been more aware. *He* wanted to control the pictures that got out and not the other way around. It pissed him off the way they used their long lenses and invaded his fucking privacy. He hadn't been prepared.

But the more he considered it, he realized Evie had thought ahead. Her outfit today had been hot. Those jeans molded to her long legs and ass, and her sexy heels weren't her usual scuffed boots. She looked every inch a pro player's girlfriend, which caused him to frown. Because Evie wasn't typically an expensively adorned female. And as much as he admired the new Evie, he had to admit he'd liked the old one as well.

"Damon, are you okay?" Bri asked more seriously.

"I'm doing the best I can. Resting a lot because my head still hurts."

"Good. Keep me posted. Love you."

"Love you, too." He disconnected the call and opened his browser, pulling up the site Bri had mentioned.

Sure enough, he and Evie were on the main page. Her body was aligned with his, bringing back the memory of her warmth and fragrant scent, and though she hadn't known it, his cock had reacted. He'd been hard as a rock, and the excuse to go find the pain patch had helped him calm the fuck down. Another glance at the picture and he saw her hand on his shoulder, the way her head tilted toward him. Yep, it looked real.

And damned if it hadn't felt real in the moment, too.

*   *   *

Evie had left Damon's, aware of the paparazzi snapping photos of her through the windshield. She'd put her sunglasses on as she walked out of the house and climbed into her car, ignoring them but knowing she'd probably opened Pandora's box and bracing herself for the fallout.

Once in the car, she'd called a friend who worked in a lab and arranged to drop off the patch she'd taken from Damon's back and asked for a quick turnaround on the results. He promised to do what he could, and she stopped at his place of work on her way home to hand over the Ziplock with the medication patch inside.

Later that morning, she sat in her home office with the names Damon had given her on a sheet of paper. Using her search browser, she began researching the people in his life, one by one. She began with the backup quarterback, because he had the most to gain by Damon's suspension, and pulled up his profile page on various social media sites, along with doing some basic research.

Gregory Emerson was the son of Dr. Lyle Emerson, the chair of Duke University School of Medicine, the top of his field in pediatric oncology. A position she assumed he hadn't achieved with ease. A little more research showed the man's mother was an investment banker at Circle One Investments, also top of the food chain. High achievers, both of them.

She gave the information some thought. Did that mean Damon's teammate was a spoiled brat in disguise? Or did he just want to make a name for himself on his own, and if so, how far would he go to do it? Or was he a legitimately good guy as Damon thought?

She made some notes just as her phone rang and she glanced at the screen. "Hi, Bri."

"Hi, my newly infamous friend."

"What do you mean?" Evie turned her attention to Damon's trainer, Jimmy O'Roarke, typing in his name.

"I mean, open up TNZ and look at the main photo on the home page."

She changed her search, her fingers flying across the keyboard, and she looked at her screen. "Oh, shit," she said, staring at a photo of herself in Damon's doorway in an extremely intimate-looking position. Only she knew she'd been checking the adhesive on his skin. To everyone else it appeared as if she was reluctant to leave and had sidled up close behind him, her face and lips close to his back and neck.

"It's actually good news. You two pulled it off. TNZ is probably figuring out who you are as we speak, and now you can go anywhere with him and it won't seem odd. Get your list together and somehow we'll try and get you to meet the people you suspect as having something to do with Damon testing positive."

"Okay." A beep signaled another call was coming in. "Bri? I need to take this call. I'll get back to you later." She disconnected and glanced at her phone, immediately taking the call. "Damon?" She was

Dare to Tempt

surprised to hear from him despite the fact that they'd exchanged numbers last night.

"Hey," he said. "I suppose you've heard the news?"

"That we're an *item*?"

"TNZ posted it on their site and every social media outlet they have a presence on. The fans took it from there. We're viral."

"And you? Did you share the information about us on your page?"

He chuckled, a low, rumbling sound. "No, I figured we can take a picture together and announce things our own way."

She laughed. "I like the sound of that." She could use some control in her life, and this would be one way of taking some back. Even if it was for the job.

A knock sounded at her door, and she walked across the apartment to answer it, wondering who would show up without calling first. She looked through the peephole, but no one was there. Frowning, she opened the door and caught sight of a box left right outside.

Still standing in her doorway, she knelt down and picked up the long box.

"So, I was thinking we could get dinner and talk about who could have framed me some more," Damon was saying as she lifted the top off the white

37

box.

"I—" A familiar spray of yellow roses, her favorite, was in the box.

John used to send her yellow roses. Before she could process that thought, a garden snake popped out of the long green stems. The unexpected sight caused her to scream and drop the box along with the phone and back away from the gift that had been clearly meant to catch her off guard.

"Evie!" she heard Damon yell from her phone.

Shit. She picked it up and spoke to him. "I'm here."

"What happened?"

"Nothing." She was a private investigator he'd hired. No reason for him to think she couldn't handle herself.

"Bullshit."

"I saw a snake," she said, figuring that would end that.

"Inside your house?" He sounded skeptical.

She bit the inside of her cheek.

"What's your address? I'm coming over."

"What? No." She didn't need hand-holding.

She'd just been shocked, which had no doubt been John's intent, but she'd moved since he'd bothered her last. And now he'd found her and the harassment was starting all over again. He resented the fact that he'd lost his job thanks to her, lost his license as an attorney, conveniently ignoring the fact that he'd physically hurt her. But he'd pulled enough strings to get himself off with some slick deal. Somehow.

"I can call Bri and get your address," he reminded her.

"You're overreacting." She glanced at the *gift*, and since the snake was still wrapped in the flower stems, she had no intention of picking it up. She quickly put the top of the box back on.

Inside she was still shaking, and she didn't doubt he heard the fear and panic in her voice. Her hand went to her arm, the reminder that John's pranks could escalate quickly.

"I'm waiting."

"Fine," she muttered and gave him her address. "It's a garden apartment. I'm on the fourth floor. Four oh two. The top floor."

"See you soon." He disconnected the call and she slammed her door shut, not wanting to give the snake the opportunity to come inside.

Either snake. Her ex or the slithering reptile outside.

*   *   *

Evie's scream still reverberated in Damon's ear, sending chills through his body. He didn't give a shit if he had concussion symptoms, he needed to get to her. He had a mother and a sister. He knew when a woman screamed in shock over a bee, a bug, or a snake. He also knew terror when he heard it. So he didn't think he was overreacting heading over to Evie's apartment. He needed to find out what had happened to cause her to shriek loudly and come back to the phone, her voice still trembling.

He pulled into a visitors' parking spot and jumped out, locking his McLaren and shoving his keys into his pocket. She lived in a pretty yellow garden apartment complex with catwalks that overlooked the parking lot. Instead of waiting for the elevator, he ran up the stairs, fuck the pain in his head, to the fourth floor and followed the signs to the left.

Her apartment was close to the elevator, and a box sat outside the door. He walked over and kicked off the top, finding yellow roses and the snake Evie had seen. At a glance, it was a harmless garden snake, but the roses were carefully packed up and delivered. The reptile hadn't gotten in there by mistake.

Ignoring the box for now, he knocked on the door. "Evie? It's me. Open up."

He heard the deadbolt unlock, and she pulled the door open, peeking through the crack before swinging it wide. She faced him, her skin pale. She'd changed from this morning's outfit into a pair of tight leggings and a hooded sweatshirt, looking more like the Evie he knew.

A pang hit him at the vulnerable way she hugged her arms around her chest.

"Come in. Watch out for the snake."

He frowned. "Get me a garbage bag," he said.

He gathered everything into the bag, let the snake go at the far side of the building into bushes that led toward a copse of trees, and he threw out the flowers in the trash chute. Then he sauntered back upstairs to find out what the hell was going on.

He found Evie curled up on the sofa, a blanket over her legs. Eyeing her warily, he walked over and sat down at the far end of the couch. "Lock the door," she said, tilting her head.

He did as she asked, making sure to flip the deadbolt, wondering if she was always this careful or if that package had triggered her.

"Want to tell me what happened?" As opposed to asking if she was okay.

Evie needed to be seen as tough, and he had no desire to prick that exterior and watch her bleed. He had too much respect for her to do that.

She swallowed hard, her slender throat moving up and down as she watched him, clearly wondering how much she wanted to reveal. "I had a bad relationship," she said, obviously reluctant to discuss her past.

"How bad?" He'd pull the information out of her piece by piece if he had to.

She worked her jaw before speaking. "Bad enough that I had to involve the police, get a restraining order, which has expired, and eventually move from my old apartment to here."

He curled his hands into fists at his sides, angry that someone would threaten any woman, but especially someone who was his to look out for. He might have fought this fake relationship in the beginning, and they might only be twenty-four hours in, but from the moment she'd sealed her lips over his, he'd felt protective of her.

He glanced her way, watching as she plucked at a thread on the blanket, her dark hair falling around her face.

"How long has this been going on?" he asked.

She raised her gaze. "It stopped after I moved six months ago."

"And what makes you so sure the *gift* was from him?" he asked, using the word with deliberate sarcasm.

"He used to buy me yellow roses. And he knows I hate snakes." She shuddered at the mention of the reptiles.

"Shit," he said, running a hand through his hair as he realized his mistake.

"What's wrong?" She shifted in her seat and stretched out her long legs.

He groaned. "I shouldn't have rushed to toss the evidence." But she'd been upset and freaked out, and he'd wanted her to feel safe. Besides, he hadn't had a heads-up that he might need to save or search the box. "Was there a note?"

"I couldn't bring myself to look. Snake, remember?" A wry smile lifted her lips.

"I think we should call the police," he said, aware at least from procedurals on television it was important to keep a record of the incident.

She shook her head. "No. This wasn't a big deal."

He leaned forward, placing a hand on her leg, her bones smaller and more delicate than his. "Evie, it's important to document the incident." In case this was just the beginning of her ex-boyfriend's campaign and he ramped up his stalking.

She sighed. "You're right. I just can't believe this is happening again. I haven't heard from him since I moved, but he's obviously decided to show up in my life again." She met his gaze. "I mean, why now?"

He hated the idea that came to mind.

She must have caught something in his expression, because she stiffened. "What are you thinking?"

"That it's no coincidence that your ex has come out of hiding now. You just went viral with a famous boyfriend."

Her eyes opened wide. "And God forbid I have a good life after I *ruined his*," she said, using air quotes. "That bastard."

If Damon got his hands on the son of a bitch, he'd kill him. "You still need to call the police."

She nodded. "I know." She took her phone off the table and dialed. "Mack? I need you to come right over. I'll explain when you get here."

Mack? Who the fuck was Mack? And why was there a sudden gnawing jealousy in Damon's gut at the thought of her calling another man?

Chapter Three

As Damon and Evie waited, she paced the floor of her cozy apartment. The place had a pretty, feminine touch, with a cream-colored sofa and bright floral pillows, matching glass cocktail and end tables in the center of the room, with watercolor paintings on the walls and a television in front of the couch.

From the way she circled the room, not meeting his gaze, he knew her revelations had her feeling vulnerable. She didn't want him to look at her as weak, and though he viewed her as tough, she'd never believe him.

She sighed and rubbed her hands on her arms. "Can I get you something to drink?"

"No, thanks, but I would like you to sit down and try to relax. Maybe we can talk some more." He wanted her to trust him, not pull away.

She joined him on the sofa, and he slid closer, the now familiar scent of her perfume a reminder of how good she'd tasted when his tongue slipped between her lips. A rush of arousal threatened and he cleared his throat, shifting in his seat. This wasn't the time or the place to react to her as a soft female.

Especially because she was eying him warily. "So, let's talk about who might want you off the playing field instead."

He leaned close and tapped her on the nose. "I know what you're doing and I'm not going to let you change the subject."

"There is no subject," she said, those luscious lips pouting.

She obviously felt more in control discussing his case than she was dealing with her own problems, but he wasn't going to let her get away with deflecting.

He cocked an eyebrow. "Your ex having a grudge against you is the subject." He glanced around the small apartment and thought about how quiet her building seemed to be. He hadn't run into anyone when he'd arrived, he'd come up by himself on the stairs and hadn't seen people waiting near the elevator. "I'm worried about you staying alone here," he said again.

"What?" Her voice rose. "I'll be fine. As you know, I have a deadbolt, and believe me, I use it. I also have a concealed-carry permit. I'll be fine."

Before he could respond, a knock sounded.

"Mack is here." She jumped up and headed to the door.

Damon followed close behind her.

Before she could look into the peephole, he heard the sound of the locks being opened, and the man let himself in, key in hand. "Jesus, Evie, what happened? You scared me when you said to come right over." He pulled her into a hug she eagerly returned.

Folding his arms across his chest, Damon stared hard at the guy he presumed was Mack, wondering what the odd feelings were flooding his system. One thing he knew, he didn't like them one bit.

"Holy shit. What's Damon Prescott doing here?" The man, who was as built and muscular as Damon himself, held out a hand. "Hey, man. Mack Wolfe. Evie's brother."

"He's a detective with the Miami PD," she said.

Damon shook his hand, his entire body relaxing at his introduction. "Good to meet you. I'm Evie's—"

"Client," she chimed in before he could say anything else, presumably like *fake boyfriend* or *real boyfriend* if he'd wanted to perpetuate the ruse even with her family.

He shut the door behind him and Evie immediately turned the deadbolt.

"Okay, what's going on? Why the panicked call?" Mack asked.

She blew out a long breath. "I received a package today."

His expression hardened. "From John?"

She nodded. "No one else can cause that kind of reaction, as you well know."

"Son of a bitch. I'm going to kill him." He curled his big hands into fists.

"What's John's last name?" Damon asked Mack because he already knew Evie wouldn't want him to know or get involved in any way.

"Coltrane," Mack said to a glaring Evie.

She glanced at Damon. "You have your own issues to worry about. I can handle my ex myself."

Mack looked from Evie to Damon and grinned. "Well, this is interesting." But he sobered quickly. "Where's the box?"

With a groan, Damon said, "I didn't know there was a stalking issue. She was upset and I tossed it."

Mack winced.

"I put it down the trash chute."

Mack pulled out his phone and asked for a patrol car to meet him at Evie's address. "We'll find it and check for a card or at least find out what florist it came from." He turned to Damon. "Now as much as I'm a fan and respect you, I want to talk to my sister."

It took everything inside Damon to walk away, but first he had something to say. "I don't think you should stay here right now," he said to Evie again, watching as a scowl took hold of her pretty face. He glanced at her brother, hoping for backup.

"The man's got a point," Mack said.

"Seriously? I can take care of myself and I'm armed. I'll be fine."

"And I have a gated community, a lot of space between neighbors, and cameras everywhere," Damon said, realizing his house was the safest place for her. "I just want you to be safe."

Mack raised an eyebrow. "Or she could move in with her brother, the cop, instead of a client she barely knows."

Clearly Mack had shifted to big-brother mode, something Damon recognized because he'd feel the same way about Bri if the situation were reversed.

"You have to work. I'm home full-time right now," Damon said, frowning at the reminder of his own situation. "Besides, I'm telling you my security system is second to none."

"Or she can think and speak for herself and stay home," Evie said to them both, her eyes flashing with annoyance. And damned if her defiance wasn't a turn-on.

"I think it's time for you both to leave. Damon, I'll keep working on your situation. Mack, I love you. Please dig into whether you can prove it was John who sent the package." She pushed her brother toward the door, and Damon understood he had no choice but to follow.

But if she thought he'd go home and pretend today hadn't happened, she was wrong. He'd be checking on her soon and often.

*   *   *

Evie shuffled the men out of her apartment, closed up and flipped the locks behind them, leaning against the door with a groan. Damn these men who thought they knew best. Yes, she understood their concern, but she wished they'd trust her to protect herself. The only reason John had gotten the best of her last time was because she'd been coming home from a party for a friend, wearing a dress without her gun, her guard down.

And though he'd frightened her today, once she gathered her wits, she trusted herself. She had to or she would lose all sense of her own identity. Ever since he'd attacked her, she'd questioned herself and her judgment. She couldn't let him get to her again or drive her out of her home.

Instead of focusing on her fear, she turned her attention to Damon's case and figuring out who had framed him. Luckily for him, she'd recently wrapped up two cases when Bri had approached her with Damon's, and she could give him her full focus.

She opened her notepad, turned on her laptop, and began looking further into his backup quarterback,

Gregory Emerson. She researched him as far back as she could, trying to get a feel for the type of person he was. A check with the police department revealed he didn't have a record. True to what Damon had said, he appeared to be a great guy, a smile always on his face, no skeletons that she could find at a surface glance.

Before she turned to her computer guy to see what else he could dig up, she wanted to make sure she was looking in the right direction. Which meant she needed to look into Damon's trainer as well.

Before she could go down that rabbit hole on her laptop, her phone rang. "Hello?"

"Hi!" Quinn's voice provided a welcome distraction. "Are we going to yoga class tonight?"

Evie winced. "I forgot." But relaxing and going for a latte with her friend after the snake incident was exactly what she needed. "But yes, let's go. Coffee shop after?"

"You know it."

She let out a relieved breath. Not only did she have a lot to tell her friend, she knew she'd feel better after getting Quinn's take on everything that was going on in Evie's life.

She didn't know what scared her more, John's resurgence, Damon's insistence that she stay with him, or the part inside her that had wanted to accept his offer. But she had her gun, she knew better than to walk around unaware, and she'd taken self-defense classes since the incident with her ex. She was as prepared as she could be and she intended to live her life.

A little while later, Evie met up with Quinn at Downward Dog, a yoga studio in downtown Miami. She caught up with her friend, who dressed similarly in leggings and a sport bra with an oversized tank top and dropped armholes. At times like this, she couldn't cover her scar and just did her best not to look at it, but she couldn't help feeling exposed and vulnerable with the reminder of her judgment lapse there for everyone to see.

They both carried their own mats, and after hugging hello, they headed inside to wait for the instructor. Not a lot of people had shown up yet for class, and they had their pick of space.

"So, how's it going with Damon's case? Did you two meet up and talk?" Quinn asked as she rolled her red mat onto the floor.

Evie did the same with her purple one. "I have ideas but nothing concrete."

"Are you two getting along?"

She lowered herself to the mat and glanced at Quinn, who sat cross-legged on the floor. "We are." All she could envision was the look on his face when he said he just wanted her to be safe.

"Hey, what aren't you telling me?" Quinn asked.

"Nothing." Evie shook her head to clear her mind, which she'd have to do soon anyway when class started.

Quinn narrowed her gaze. "Then what's with that dreamy expression on your face, hmm?"

"I'm just thinking, that's all." She lengthened her legs out in front of her and bent forward, stretching her muscles.

"Thinking about a dark-haired, indigo-eyed, sexy athlete?"

"Just because you fell for Austin, don't put those fairy-tale dreams on me. I'm just fine on my own." A glance at the scar on her arm reminded her of that fact, even if the tingle in her lower regions contradicted her. Every time she looked at Damon, her body came alive. Not that she'd admit as much to her best friend, who just happened to be his soon-to-be sister-in-law.

"Okay, ladies, let's get started." Nadia, their instructor, walked into the room, and for the next hour, between Downward Dog and Shavasana, Evie forgot everything and managed to relax and put everything out of her mind.

Until she and Quinn sat down at their favorite coffee shop, their lattes in hand. She'd asked for decaf because the last thing she needed was to be hopped up and awake all night. It was just past dinnertime and she planned to reheat something later at home.

"What's going on? For someone so outgoing, you've been quiet. You know you can talk to me, right?" Quinn leaned in, her green eyes focused on Evie's face.

She bit the inside of her cheek, despite knowing she was going to tell her best friend everything. She just didn't find it easy, and Quinn knew her well enough to wait her out.

Wrapping her hand around the warm cup, she stared at the white cover and finally decided she was ready to explain. "John found me today. He sent a gift."

"Dammit." Quinn looked at her with worried eyes. "Tell me what happened?"

Evie reiterated the entire story, including Mack's idolization of Damon and, more reluctantly, Damon's offer for her to stay with him.

"No kidding? Damon the bachelor wants you to move in?" Quinn grinned. "I love it."

"It's not like that. He was worried about my safety." And Evie would keep telling herself that because to think otherwise was dangerous.

"Right. And he could have offered to pay for you to stay at a hotel and he didn't. Damon doesn't bring women home, which tells me he's invested," Quinn said, looking proud of her conclusions.

"After one night of play dating?" Evie let out a noise of disbelief. "He was being … chivalrous."

Quinn's smile grew wider. "Another word I wouldn't have associated with Damon." She took a sip of her coffee.

"Back to the flowers, you're sure it's John?" Quinn asked.

Running her hand over the smooth wooden table, Evie thought about the afternoon. "Mack didn't find a card with the flowers and the flowers were in a plain white box. I wanted to dig, but he insisted it was his job."

"As your brother or as a detective?" Quinn raised an eyebrow.

Chuckling, Evie said, "A little bit of both." Even though it killed her to take a step back in her own life and investigation, she'd let her brother handle it. "You know, Damon thinks John surfaced now because we went viral in that picture and he's jealous. I have a life and he doesn't. We know he blames me, but it was his fault he lost his law license, his job, his marriage. Not mine." Her hand squeezed the cup too tight and the top popped off. At least she'd drunk enough coffee so it didn't spill.

"So Damon knows everything about John?" Quinn asked pointedly.

Evie shook her head. "Not everything." She not-so-absently rubbed the scar on her arm. "That's on a need-to-know business and he doesn't need to know. I'm just hoping that with that one prank, John got his digs in and he's done with me."

"I hope so."

But they both knew that wasn't true. It wasn't in her ex's nature to give up.

"So, how's that adorable baby?" Evie changed the subject to Quinn's favorite topic.

"Jenny is so cute! She knows my voice and turns toward me when she hears me. And she smiles at us. Close to a laugh."

Her eyes lit up as she described the baby that had been left on Austin's doorstep and turned out to be his. He'd asked Quinn, who'd been his assistant at the time, to move in and help, and they'd fallen in love. Which effectively made her Jenny's mother since the baby's biological mom had signed away her parental rights.

"And I want to go shopping this weekend for furniture. She can't stay in a Pack 'n Play forever and we need to make her room into a nursery."

"Sounds great. I'm thrilled for you. You know that, right?" If anyone deserved happiness, it was Quinn. She always did things for others. As a child, she'd helped her parents raise her siblings, and she was the perfect executive assistant. She hadn't planned on a family of her own, but now that she had one, she literally glowed with happiness.

Evie expected Austin to propose any day now and she knew Quinn would say yes. Because happily ever after was in the cards for some people. Just not for Evie. Damon was a job and she intended to handle it and him well.

*   *   *

Evie drove home, more aware of her surroundings than she'd ever been before, hyper-focused and more alert than since she'd moved and tried to put John behind her. She left her car and locked it, heading inside. She kept a hand on her hip, where she could easily reach her gun, and walked into the lobby, taking the elevator to her floor.

Soon she was back in her apartment, where she locked up tight and closed her shades. One more incident and she planned to ask the landlord's permission to install an alarm. She didn't want to overreact in case John had just been looking for one last-ditch opportunity to frighten her with the flowers and the snake. If he was on a mission of terror, she needed every means of keeping him out.

Pushing those thoughts out of her head she ate some quick leftovers. Then she took a shower, wrapped her hair into a bun, and slid on her favorite soft-as-butter tank top and panties.

Instead of obsessing, she took out her headphones and pulled up an app her yoga instructor had recommended for sleep and stress, headphones being an important part of the meditation and sounds.

Then she lay down, turned on the soothing voice, and followed the instructions, getting lost in her breathing and the calming exercises. As usual, when it ended, she pulled off the headphones and rolled over, immediately falling into a deep sleep.

She woke when she heard what she thought was the building's fire alarm going off. The sun was just beginning to peek through the sides of the window.

Since it wasn't a normal occurrence, she rushed out of bed, pulled on a pair of jeans, slipped her flip-flops on, grabbed her phone, her keys, tucked her gun into the back of her pants, and left her apartment. Once in the hall, her neighbors exited en masse as well. They walked the four flights down the stairs and crossed the parking lot to stand outside just as fire trucks and police sirens alerted them to their arrival.

*   *   *

Damon woke up at seven a.m. He'd left his phone in the kitchen last night, crashing early thanks to his head, and when he walked in to make a smoothie, he picked up the cell and pressed the side button. A stream of messages from Austin poured in, each one more annoyed than the last. The gist of it was to call his brother back, and Damon's gut churned because it obviously wasn't good news.

He tapped his brother's name on the screen and waited for him to answer, which he did on the first ring.

"Hey, bro. What's up?" Damon asked.

"Where the fuck have you been? I called you all night."

Damon winced at the frustration in Austin's voice. "I shut my phone off. Sorry." He drew a deep breath. "I lost the appeal, didn't I?"

"I'm sorry, Damon."

His stomach tumbled at the news.

"We knew it was a long shot," Austin was saying. "Without being able to argue the validity of the testing, we never really had a chance. They don't call it a zero-tolerance policy for no reason."

"Yeah." Disappointment and rage warred within him. Even though he hadn't done anything wrong, the suspension resulted in him letting his team down and he hated it.

"I'm out four games beginning with the start of the season. In a contract year." He didn't give a shit about the money penalty. Just about letting everyone down.

"Breathe, Damon. Ian knows you. He won't base the contract offer on this situation."

Damon ran a hand through his hair. "Ian has a salary cap and the reputation of himself and the team to worry about."

"And we have Evie. Give her a call. Regroup. Come up with a plan. At least you'll feel proactive."

"Yeah," he muttered. "I'd rather drink myself stupid."

"Except it's seven in the morning, not to mention it's not good for your body or your concussion. Just calm down and we'll deal with this. I promise."

"Thanks." Damon disconnected the call, feeling sick. Knowing what and who he needed, he picked up the phone and texted Evie.

* * *

As Evie waited outside with her neighbors, she glanced at her phone. A little after seven a.m. It buzzed and she turned it over, glancing at the screen to see a text from Damon.

Damon: *Morning, sunshine.*

She grinned and texted back: *Morning* ☺

Damon: *Checking in.*

Evie: *I'm fine. Gas leak at my building. Standing out-*

side.

Damon: *Keep an eye out around you. I'm coming.*

She wanted to roll her eyes, but she couldn't. She'd grabbed her gun for just the possibility that John decided to mix into the crowd.

No need to come, she typed, but there was no *read* confirmation beneath the words.

Her stomach flipped at the possibility of seeing him, and she lectured herself about how crazy those unwanted feelings were. He was a client. She couldn't let herself give in, because she'd sworn off men after she'd misjudged John so badly.

"Evie! Evie!" her brother Mack yelled, finding her in the crowd.

"Mack!" She waved and he met up on the grass. "What's wrong in the building? Do you know?" she asked, realizing he'd probably heard the news on his police scanner.

"Someone called in a gas leak," her brother said.

She blinked. "That could be serious." She lowered her voice. "The building could explode."

He nodded. "The fire department is setting up near the fire hydrant and going in with meters. Meanwhile, the police are moving you all back farther," he said, just as a uniformed officer directed them far from the building.

"Is Deke here?" she asked of her brother the firefighter.

"I haven't seen him yet but he's on shift. I'm sure he's around somewhere." Mack glanced over people's heads.

Evie patted his shoulder. "Why don't you go see what you can find out?"

"Good idea. Stay put." He kissed her forehead and strode off, leaving Evie to wait … for Damon.

*   *   *

Once again, Damon found himself driving too fast to Evie's apartment, concern gnawing at his gut. At least his symptoms were lessening. He didn't know why he felt the need to rush over. Gas leaks happened, and most likely they'd clear things out and let them back into the building.

He parked far from the building and the crowds and made his way toward the people who were probably tenants. He glanced around the group, looking for Evie, which wasn't difficult given his six-foot-four height. He saw her face peeking out from the side, while a large man in a firefighter uniform had her in a bear hug. Damon's stomach twisted with what he acknowledged was jealousy, and he strode up to them just as the man released her.

She turned. He stared, taking her in at a glance.

Wearing a pair of tight jeans and a tank top, her nipples poking through the thin fabric, she was his every dream come to life, and his twitching cock let him know it.

"Evie," he said in a gruff voice.

"Damon!" She appeared happy to see him, her smile warm and welcoming.

He glanced at the other man, who, now that he turned around, looked very much like Mack, from his dark hair to his brown eyes and facial features.

"Let me guess. Another brother?" he asked, the relief running through him intense.

Evie grinned. "Deke, this is—"

"Damon Prescott! Hey, man, what an honor!" Deke extended his hand and Damon shook it. "What are you doing here?"

"He's a client."

Deke's brows furrowed in confusion, no doubt because there was no reason for a client to be here this early and especially during an evacuation.

It was time for Damon and Evie to have a talk about their status. If she was his fake girlfriend, she needed to act like it all the time. And since their kiss had been impulsive and not in front of an audience, they definitely needed to nail down what was going on between them. Damon knew what he wanted. To see where things between them could go. In the real world.

Deke lifted his helmet and scratched his head. "I'd love to talk and hear more, but now that I know Evie's out of her apartment and safe, I need to get back to work."

He shot Evie a look that Damon interpreted as *I want an explanation for Damon Prescott coming over at this hour later.*

"Bye, Deke. Be careful." She watched him leave, concern etched on her face.

Damon didn't like seeing her worried or upset. "He'll be fine."

She nodded. "I know. It's his job and he's good at it. He knows how to be careful."

He studied her makeup-free face, realizing she was as beautiful with all the artifice as without. In fact, he liked seeing her olive skin glowing and her lips bare. He'd love to devour them and see how she tasted without fake goop on her lips.

He shoved his hands into his jean pockets. "So, any more brothers I should know about?"

She grinned. "Lucas is an EMT and Joshua is a mechanic."

He let out a low whistle. That would teach him not to jump to conclusions every time she hugged another man. "Must have been hard bringing boyfriends home."

She chuckled. "They had to be pretty damn brave to face the four of them, plus my dad." She met his gaze.

"Are they still tough on the guys in your life?" Because he wanted to be her guy. He knew that now.

Driving over here, worrying about her again, he had a sudden rush of certainty. They deserved a real shot. His life sucked and he wanted her to be there while he went through it. He suddenly understood Austin more. How being with Quinn after his infant daughter, Jenny, had arrived, seeing her in a new light, sent his one-time bachelor brother into a man determined to make Quinn his.

Still, the reminder of losing his appeal sent his mood crashing to the ground. "Oh, by the way, I lost the appeal. My suspension remains intact," he said low enough no one could overhear.

"Oh, Damon. I'm sorry." Without warning, she stepped forward and pulled him into a hug.

One he hadn't known he'd needed. Her warm body pressed into his, her breasts crushing against his chest, the thin material of her top hardly a barrier. Her nipples were hard and tight, and his hands slid to her waist, his palms brushing her bare skin. He felt the gun she'd tucked into her jeans and was glad she'd thought to protect herself.

Someone jostled against them and she stepped

back, looking up at him with heat in her eyes. He experienced the same warmth sizzling through his veins.

"Do you want to talk about it?" she asked quietly, not acknowledging the moment, instead leading him away from the group of people.

Some pointed but nobody had bothered him for an autograph or photo, probably because they'd all just rolled out of bed. Not the best selfie moment.

He drew a deep breath. "About the suspension. It doesn't just suck, it's devastating. I can live with letting myself down because I know I didn't do it. I can focus on who has it in for me and why. But my team? They need me and it's a quarter of the season. They don't deserve to be let down by their quarterback." He shook his head, looking down at the dewy grass.

"Those who know you will trust you," she assured him, slipping her hand into his and squeezing tight.

He appreciated her show of support and wrapped his larger fingers around hers. "Yeah, but that doesn't change the fact that I'm out for four games."

"I understand," she murmured.

"There's something else." He heard himself speak and was shocked at what he was about to reveal to her. "Now that it's official and there's no way out, I hear my father's voice in my head."

She narrowed her gaze. "So, Quinn told me last

year that Austin donated a kidney to your uncle Paul, who admitted to being your real father."

"Sperm donor dad." A wry smile lifted his lips. "I love that man. Growing up, when my dad was an asshole, Uncle Paul was always the voice of reason. But now? I imagine Jesse's disappointment. I can hear him berating me for not being good enough, for letting my teammates down. And it sucks."

She sighed. "I won't minimize your feelings and I can't take them away. I can only tell you that we'll figure this out, and though it won't bring back the games you miss, at least you'll have validation. I'm going to do my best for you."

"I'm grateful." Even though she was being paid to do a job, those brown eyes looking up at him with faith told him she was invested in more than a paycheck. Which was a good thing, because he was becoming equally invested in her.

*   *   *

Evie and Damon remained outside for another hour while the firefighters cleared the building. Mack stopped by to explain that the superintendent was taking the firemen through the apartments, letting them check each one with gas meters before declaring the building all clear.

Her conversation with Damon about his father lay

on her mind, as did his feelings about letting his teammates down. She couldn't help but feel like Emerson getting his opportunity to prove himself meant something to this investigation. But she hadn't brought up the backup quarterback's name to Damon again this morning, not wanting to rub salt in an open wound.

Finally, someone began to speak through a megaphone, announcing it was safe to go back inside.

She glanced at Damon. "I appreciate you keeping me company. Stay for breakfast?" she asked. Although she knew he was a client, she also wasn't ready for him to leave yet. That fired-up moment between them earlier stayed with her.

Her need to offer comfort, her arms wrapped around his, the musky smell of man, and the heat in his eyes afterwards. She didn't want a relationship, dammit, but she couldn't turn her back on him when he was at his lowest.

"Are you cooking?" he asked.

She broke into a grin. "You don't know me that well but no. I'm ordering in from my favorite pancake place."

His hot gaze slid over her. She already knew what it felt like to rub against that muscular body and how much she'd both enjoyed the feeling and wanted more.

"I'm not sure where you put the carbs, but damn,

you wear it well."

She flushed at his admiration.

"Count me in since I'm not exactly in training at the moment," he said, unaware of the pleasure his compliment gave her. "I can afford a cheat." He frowned and she hated that she'd reminded him of his suspension.

"Come on up. I'll call in the order."

He nodded. "Give me a minute. I want to talk to your brother and see what they found."

"Okay." She smiled and headed in along with everyone else from her building.

*   *   *

Damon waited until she'd gone inside and strode to where the fire engine sat idle and looked around for Evie's brothers. He caught sight of Mack and called out his name.

The man turned and strode over to Damon. "Hey."

"Hey."

Mack narrowed his gaze. "I know you didn't sleep here, but you're here at the ass crack of dawn. Am I right in thinking there's more between you and Evie than client and PI?"

Admiring his blunt assessment and the fact that he didn't give a shit about Damon's fame, Damon decided to answer with respect and not a smart-ass *none of your business* comment.

"I like your sister," he said.

"Define like."

Like, now it was none of his fucking business, Damon thought, but didn't say it. "Like I want to get to know her better." He doubted Mack was aware of Damon's nonexistent dating history.

Hookups? Yes. Dating? No.

Because he'd watched his mother stay with a man who'd been a dick to her kids, Damon hadn't ever thought he'd find someone who would make him want to try for more than a night or two max. He couldn't say he'd seen a loving relationship growing up. His mom spent her time making sure she was a buffer between her husband and children. Austin hadn't gotten the brunt of Jesse Prescott's wrath as he was more of the natural athlete. Although Damon knew Austin thought Damon hadn't had it that bad, Damon had built his own resentments toward their father. But Evie? She was complex and unique, and she made him want to know her on a deeper, more emotional level.

Mack digested Damon's comment, his intent, and puffed out his chest. "You know what I'm going to say, right?"

Damon squared his shoulders. "I have a sister, which means, yes, I know exactly what you're going to say. And I'm not going to hurt her," he said preemptively. If anything, he'd been more open and honest with Evie in a short time than with any other woman ever.

Watching him warily, Mack said, "Good, because I don't care how famous you are, she's got four brothers willing to kick your ass if you do."

"Point made," Damon reassured the man. "Now about the gas leak. What did they find?"

Mack looked toward the truck, where the guys were wrapping things up. "Nothing. Not a damn thing as far as I know."

Just then, Deke strode over, a sheen of sweat on his face from wearing his uniform in the Florida heat. "What's up?" he asked, looking from Damon to Mack.

Mack shrugged. "Just warning the famous athlete to watch himself with Evie or he'll have us to answer to."

Before Damon could respond to that, Mack asked, "You and your guys find anything?"

Deke, who'd begun to look Damon over, shook his head. "Either the call to 911 about a gas leak was a false alarm or a prank."

"A prank." Damon frowned. Something felt off to him about it being a hoax, what with Evie's asshole ex roaming around, but he wasn't about to tell her brothers and have them hovering even more. Not when gut instinct was all he had.

"Hey, Wolfe!" another firefighter called out, joining them. "Did you see an unfamiliar-looking guy wearing one of our uniforms lurking around?" he asked Deke.

Damon narrowed his gaze while Mack jerked to alertness.

"What do you mean?" Deke asked.

A young guy, younger than Damon at twenty-five, lifted his hat and ran a hand through his hair. "An old woman said she asked one of us to make sure we didn't let her cat out of her apartment when we did the door-to-door checks. Told him to come back and let her know her apartment was safe. She was frantic. Probably age related, you know? Anyway, she saw the guy again after and called out to him, but he ignored her. Instead he got into a car and drove away. She was giving Chief an earful when I saw you guys and walked over here."

"You come and go in the truck only, right?" Mack asked.

The new guy nodded. "Any of you see anything odd? Deke, you see anyone unfamiliar?"

"No." He folded his arms across his chest and looked at the men milling around the front of the building and the engine.

"Motherfucker," Damon muttered. "That bastard

has something to do with this, I'm sure."

Deke jerked his head around. "Who?"

With a groan, Mack spoke. "John, Evie's ex."

Deke's eyes opened wide. "What the fuck? That bastard surfaced again?"

A loud whistle sounded. "Come on, Wolfe, Holmes. Haul ass. We're out of here," someone called from nearby.

Deke glared at his brother. "I've got to go but you owe me an explanation." He and his fellow firefighter jogged over to the truck, whose engine had already been started.

"You didn't tell him about the gift?" Damon asked.

Mack flushed a deep red. "Didn't want him freaking out, but I'll get him, Josh, and Lucas together and explain."

Damon's gut twisted with dread. "I've got to get upstairs."

"And I'm going to find out more about this supposed firefighter," Mack said. "Keep an eye on her," he instructed Damon.

As if he planned to do anything else.

Chapter Four

Evie hadn't asked Damon what he wanted for breakfast, but his eyes had lit up at the idea of pancakes, so she ordered her favorites. The restaurant knew her by name and was aware of her usual order. Apple pancakes, chocolate chip pancakes, because she liked both and always had one of each, and an order of plain just in case Damon didn't want to share what she'd chosen.

She washed up quickly and changed into a pair of sweats and a long-sleeve shirt. Damon hadn't noticed the scar yet, and she didn't want to have to get into an explanation now. She set the table and had just finished when Damon knocked. She heard his voice telling her it was him from outside.

Opening the door, she let him in. He looked around, frazzled. "What's wrong?" she asked.

"Is everything okay?" He looked behind her.

She blinked in surprise. "Of course. Why?"

He shut the door behind him and locked it. He hesitated and she frowned.

"Just tell me what's wrong." She hated suspense.

"I was talking to your brothers. They thought this whole situation was either a false alarm or a prank. Then one of the firefighters told Deke that there was a man who was pretending to be one of them. And after mixing in and I assume getting into the building, he left in his car, not in the fire engine like the rest of the guys."

Her heart skipped a beat at the implication. "You think it was John?"

"We don't know but it's a possibility."

"That stupid son of a bitch."

"The problem is that you have no proof he's stalking you, which means you can't get a restraining order," Damon muttered.

"He's good at stalking. And cheating." But she wasn't going to let John ruin her morning. "Can we stop talking about something I can't change? I'm sure Mack is going to end up having someone drive by here often if he doesn't do it himself."

He looked like he wanted to argue … or say something more, but as if she'd summoned the food, her bell rang. Damon strode there first and looked through the peephole before opening the door and accepting the package, discovering she'd already paid and tipped with an app.

"I would have paid for your breakfast," he said as she took the bag from him.

She smiled. "I know. And I can afford to treat you." She unpacked the Styrofoam holders and moved the pancakes onto plates, setting them on the table with maple syrup and utensils.

They sat next to each other at her kitchen table. Sun streamed in from a nearby window as they each took their choice of pancakes.

Damon took the plain kind and she wrinkled her nose at his unimaginative choice.

"Come on, don't you want a taste of chocolate chip or apple pancake? They're so good," she urged, taking a bite of chocolate chip herself.

She moaned at the taste of the chocolate and syrup sliding down her throat. At the sound, his gaze locked on hers, and she gulped down the end of the piece she'd eaten, then lowered her fork and placed it down.

He leaned in close. "Know what I like the best about pancakes?" he asked.

"What?"

"The maple syrup," he said and licked her sticky lips. He groaned as he swiped his tongue over her bottom lip, followed by her upper, then darted across the seam. A sensual request to be let inside.

She parted her mouth and tasted heaven. He kissed her thoroughly, as if afraid he'd miss one bit of the syrup, but the longer he lingered, the more she knew he was devouring *her*. And she liked it.

One hand came to rest at her neck as he tilted his head and thrust his tongue in deeper. She moaned and kissed him back, her body pulsing with desire. She'd never felt such honest emotion in a kiss before, and she didn't want it to end.

When a ring sounded, she was sure she was just lost in sensation, but the sound continued.

He leaned back, breaking their connection. "It's your cell," he said gruffly.

She glanced up at him. His lips were damp from their intense kiss. "Can I ignore it?"

He chuckled, the sound low and deep. "It's up to you."

She glanced at her phone and hit accept immediately. "Hello?"

"Evie? It's Gavin at MSP Laboratories."

She looked at Damon, who'd returned to eating his pancakes, but didn't tell him who was on the other end. "Hi. What did you find out?" she asked Gavin, who she'd gone to college with. They'd met living in the same dorm, but his classes hadn't overlapped with her criminal justice major.

"Nothing in that pain patch but lidocaine, capsaicin, methyl salicylate, and menthol. All standard ingredients."

Dammit. Although the results didn't rule out the trainer completely, she'd hoped the answer would be simple.

"Thanks, Gavin. You know where to bill me."

She disconnected the call and met Damon's gaze, putting her phone down on the table.

"Bad news," he said, not even bothering with a question.

She nodded. "There's no banned substance in the pain patch. Just the things you'd expect. I'm sorry."

"And the hits keep coming." He groaned and pushed his plate away. A waste of delicious pancakes, she thought sadly.

"Hey." She put her hand over his. "It was a long shot. There's still a lot of ground left to cover."

He treated her to a forced smile, and she decided to change the subject, not that he'd like this one any better. "So … that kiss."

To her shock, his smile grew wider and more genuine. "What about it?"

She swallowed hard, but she'd never backed away from honesty when it was important. "You're my client."

"And?"

"And we're pretending to be together and there's nobody around now to impress or prove anything to. So, what's going on?" Because she honestly didn't understand. "Up until a couple of days ago, you barely tolerated me."

"Hey, that's not true."

She raised an eyebrow. "We certainly didn't click."

"Because I didn't know you then."

She sighed. "Damon, let's be real. You all but said I'm not your type. Hell, I had to dress up just to prove to you that I could pull it off."

He frowned at that. "I'm an asshole. And I was wrong. I always thought you were gorgeous but I didn't *see* you."

"And you do now."

Reaching out, he pulled a strand of her hair, sliding it back and forth between his fingers. "Yes, I do."

"Well, you don't do relationships and neither do I. Not anymore." He didn't argue the point, so she went on. "Not to mention the fact that we have important people in common. It would be stupid to let things go any further."

Quinn, her best friend in the world, was with his brother. Evie didn't ever want to make her choose.

"I didn't say anything about a relationship. It was a kiss. A damn good kiss and one I want to repeat. And so do you." He tugged on her hair. "And as far as Quinn and Austin are concerned, we're adults. Whatever happens between us, I'm sure we can handle it without pulling them into it."

She couldn't concentrate, not with how he was lightly tugging on her hair, the feel surprisingly arousing. "You're suggesting we … what?"

"See where things go and have fun."

Could she do that? Just give in, let go, and enjoy? Didn't she deserve some good in her life for as long as it lasted?

"Stop thinking so hard," he said, leaning in close, his forehead touching hers.

"Okay."

"Well, okay then." A slow, sexy grin lifted his lips, one she couldn't resist.

And now she didn't have to.

*   *   *

Damon left Evie at her door with a deep kiss that had his cock hard and his body aching for more. More seemed to be the theme of things right now. For the first time, he wanted more from a woman than she wanted from him. Because of her hesitancy, he'd let her believe he desired a short-term, fun fling, because if he'd even hinted that he was quickly becoming invested, she'd run far and fast. She didn't trust readily and for good reason.

But for Damon, Evie was a beacon of light in a dark time in his life. He knew now that the fake girlfriend aspect wouldn't work. He'd been counting on the idea of winning his appeal and her being able to meet his teammates and others with whom he had daily contact. Now he was banned from the stadium. From doing anything that might make the NFL think he was viewing plays, watching practice, having contact with team personnel. The list went on.

He thought back to his initial conversation with his brother and realized Austin had known all along what the end result would be. Bri had, too. Damon hadn't wanted to face or hear it, and they'd offered him Evie as a PI who could play his girlfriend and assess the people around him. But that idea was now dead in the water.

Of course, there were still times they might run into people, and he knew Evie would look and play the part to the hilt. But as far as reality was concerned, he was relying on her private investigator skills to dig deep and help him find out who had set him up.

And he believed she'd do just that.

He pulled his McLaren into his garage, put the car in park, and shut the engine. As he disarmed the alarm and walked inside, his mind was back on his career. Damon didn't know whether to be relieved his trainer hadn't tried to dose his pain patch or pissed he still didn't know who had it in for him.

He just wanted a fucking answer.

*   *   *

After another day of rest and losing his mind, Damon

eyed the weights in his basement longingly but knew better than to test his concussion by working out. Not when he was slowly getting better, his head hurting less, the dizziness decreasing. Evie had checked in, assuring him she was working, but hadn't been specific as to how she was handling her investigation into who had framed him.

Considering what she now had to deal with personally, he admired her focus on her cases, because he assumed he wasn't the only client she had. He'd asked her if she'd had any further issues or contact with her ex, and she'd assured him she hadn't, which didn't stop him from thinking or worrying about her.

He wasn't used to being concerned about a woman he was involved with. Had never been emotionally attached to anyone he'd dated in his past. Hell, he hadn't thought about anything but excelling on the field, and that had taken a lot of work in the gym and out, studying tapes, talking to coaches, and running plays. But he'd never expected to find a woman who understood his life and he hadn't cared. Because nobody had gotten under his skin.

Until Evie.

Despite this being a disastrous time in his career, he couldn't stop thinking about her. Her light brown gaze, lit up with smart-ass laughter or opened in panic, stayed with him. He wished all he could think about was her sexy body or the taste of her lips. That would tell him it was a casual thing. Instead he kept wondering how she was feeling, if she was frightened, or whether she was okay after the resurgence of her ex.

Although he'd never admit it, Damon had looked up Evie's ex, Googling for information, a search that revealed John's arrest. No mention of stalking afterwards. Damon's stomach churned at the details that Evie hadn't mentioned, including a knife wound. As for John, he'd been arrested but had cut a deal, not serving time. He had, however, lost his law license and his job as, ironically, a defense attorney.

Damon tucked the information away. The only way he wanted to know more was if he heard it from Evie herself. He refused to admit he'd dug into things and violated her privacy. Despite the fact that her assault was public record, she deserved to have the dignity of telling him herself.

The photo of John Coltrane showed a clean-cut lawyer. He didn't strike Damon as Evie's type. Then again, having seen Evie dressed up and dressed down, he couldn't imagine what her type was, though he was beginning to hope it was him.

He shut the lights off in his home gym and walked back to the kitchen, pulling out a premade smoothie and taking a drink. He found comfort in routine, something he'd learned as a kid. He'd had to considering his father had been a grade-A asshole when Damon hadn't measured up to Austin. The physicality of football hadn't come naturally to Damon as it had to his oldest brother, but the mental aspect of quarterbacking clicked for him.

But the mind hadn't interested Jesse Prescott. Only the ability to take a hit on the field had. Over time, Damon learned to merge the two, and his dad, an almost-NFL player who had lost his chance due to injury in college, wanted to live through his sons. If Damon couldn't make a play, Jesse forced him to pay for it. As punishment, he'd walked home in more blazing Florida heat, cooler weather, and rainstorms than he cared to remember. He'd hated the bastard.

And last year he'd learned Jesse wasn't his biological father. He was none of the Prescott kids' biological father. In an unbelievable revelation, when their Uncle Paul had needed a kidney transplant, he'd come to them and asked them all to be tested as possible matches. Because Paul had been their sperm donor when Jesse couldn't get his wife pregnant. Another failure in Jesse's eyes. Another reason to drive his kids even harder.

Damon frowned at the memory. Austin had been the kidney donor. Damon loved his brother, but he'd always been blessed in a way that either things came easily, like football, or he was the savior, in the case of uncle Paul.

His phone rang and he glanced at the screen, seeing it was Evie. "Hello?"

"Hi. I have an idea. I know you're suspended, but you said we could run into your teammates in public places, right?"

He heard the excitement in her voice. "Right."

"I think we should go out as a couple. A place where you think your backup quarterback might be. I'd like to meet him and assess him for myself."

"I like that plan." Once the season began in earnest, the guys would basically be on lockdown, but right now? They had a chance. "I know exactly where to find Emerson."

"Where?"

"Diamond Joe's. It's a huge step down from All-stars. Less privacy and more clinging women," Damon said.

"Diamond Joe's. Oh, joy," she muttered, recognizing the name. "What's the dress code?"

"T and A," he said, laughing to himself, although from the groan on the other end of the phone, he could envision Evie rolling her eyes.

"I'll drive in case your head hurts. Pick you up at ten?" she said more than asked.

"Yes, boss," he said with a grin.

*   *   *

Damon was ready when Evie pulled up to his house in her Mini Cooper convertible. He locked up and headed out to meet her. He'd turned off his phone, wanting to give her his full attention tonight.

She opened her door and met him on the driveway, taking his breath away. A black leather miniskirt hit high on her thighs, a pair of red stilettos—fuck-me heels and he imagined doing just that—showed off her long, tanned legs, and a low-dipped shirt beneath her leather jacket revealed full, mouthwatering cleavage. God, this woman affected him. Not only did he desire her but he liked her witty mouth and smart mind. He was no longer content to look and not touch. Somehow, he had to convince her they were good together for real.

"Looking good, Evie." He dragged his gaze over hers once more.

She grinned. "Glad I meet with your approval," she said, but her eyes flashed with pleasure. "So, I thought maybe you'd want me to drive your car. Mine's a little small for you."

His head was much better today and hadn't acted up tonight. He recalled curling up in her small front seat the other night and winced. "You want to drive my McClaren." He burst out laughing.

"I can handle it. You think I can't?" She held out her hand. "Keys?"

He shook his head. "I woke up this morning finally feeling better. And I have driven when it was an emergency. I just said okay to you driving over because I wanted to make sure I was fine tonight, too." He reached into his pants pocket and pulled out his fob. "Park your car in one of the extra spots and I'll pull out."

"You're such a man." Frowning at him, she walked around her car and slid inside, starting the engine so she could move the vehicle.

"Drive my baby," he muttered, laughing as he headed back inside to open the electric door.

He backed his car out of the garage, climbing out and meeting Evie at the passenger side, opening the door for her. She slid in, the scent of her perfume hitting him hard as she brushed past him.

On the trip downtown, she peppered him with more questions about his life in an attempt to learn more about him before they met up with people he knew at the bar, and he enjoyed answering her questions.

"Who's your best friend?"

That one was easy and plural. "My brothers."

"Besides family," she said.

He glanced over at her before refocusing on the road. "Asher Dare."

She slid those long legs to the side and leaned in

close. "*The* Asher Dare? The one who, along with his brother Harrison, owns Dirty Dare Vodka? Harrison Dare, the biggest actor on the planet?"

Hands on the wheel, he grinned. "And Nick and Zach, the other brothers, and me. I have a small stake in the company as well. And yes, we're all related. And they have a sister, Emery."

She smacked her head against the back of the seat. "I never put it together."

"Why would you? They're cousins on my New York family's side."

"Why go into the vodka business?" she asked.

"When the guys decided to form the company, I'd just signed my first contract." He shrugged. "Couldn't think of anything better to do than go into the start-up with family."

She twisted toward him, obviously interested, and he continued.

Although he spoke to the guys often and they wanted to come by and commiserate, Damon had been too wrapped up in his issues to hang with his buds. Still, he knew the guys wouldn't take no for an answer much longer.

She let out a low whistle. "Your family holds some pretty impressive people, even considering who *you* are."

He chuckled and pulled into the parking lot of the

closest hotel to the bar with a valet. He'd rather walk an extra block than leave his car outside. Was the price of his vehicle ridiculous? Hell yes. But a man had to have one vice and an expensive car was his.

After settling things with the valet, he wrapped an arm around Evie's waist and they headed toward the bar. And damned if she didn't feel good and right by his side.

He held open the door and they stepped into the dimly lit tavern-looking establishment. It never failed. As people realized a celebrity was in the house, they went quiet and then the whispering began.

"You always cause such a stir?" Evie asked.

He didn't like it but it was part and parcel of the life he'd chosen. "That's why I prefer Allstars," he told her. "People have more respect for privacy. Come on. I see Emerson and a bunch of other guys on the team."

He gestured to a table where a bunch of his teammates sat with cleat chasers hanging all over them.

"Jesus, there's more boobs than clothing," Evie muttered, causing Damon to grin. "I thought the term groupie was a cliché but apparently not."

He shrugged, too used to the sight to be affected. "It's part of the life."

One wink and he could have his choice, including the same chick he'd gone home with when drunk one night. Candy? Connie? Ronnie? He groaned, hoping there wouldn't be an issue. She seemed preoccupied with Drew Brown at the moment.

It was a sad fact that any of the females at that table would leave with him if he asked. But they only desired him as a trophy. So they could say they'd slept with Damon Prescott. And the more deluded ones? They hoped for more. Evie, on the other hand, had substance.

"Is it part of the life for you, too?" she asked, a hint of snark in her tone.

"Why do you want to know? Jealous?" he asked, hugging her tighter to him.

"You wish," she muttered, and he thought she was right.

Maybe he wanted her to care.

"I'm just trying to figure out how many hearts you broke and if any of the women in your past could have drugged you to get back at you," Evie explained.

He paused halfway across the room, stopping before they could be overheard. "I don't lead women on." It was important that she believe him. "Which means none of them have a reason to punish me for something."

Before she could reply, someone bellowed, "Prescott, come join us!"

"Here goes nothing," he muttered and led her to

the table where his teammates waited.

"Who's the babe?" Emerson asked, chugging a beer after he spoke.

Damon frowned. "Watch how you speak to her," he warned his teammate. "Evie Wolfe, this is my—" He caught himself before saying backup. "This is Gregory Emerson, one of our quarterbacks. You already met Devon and James at Allstars." He continued around the table with three more players, all nodding hello. "Guys, my … girlfriend, Evie."

That pronouncement caused an uproar. Not from the two men who'd seen him with Evie at Allstars, but between Greg Emerson, Drew Brown, and the women who were looking Evie up and down, clearly finding her unworthy, everyone else had something to say.

"Her?" Candy, Mandy, or whatever looked at Evie with a scowl on her face.

Damon stiffened at the implied insult.

"Do you have a problem?" Evie asked, standing up for herself.

He was proud of her, but she didn't need to get into it with one of his past mistakes.

Damon shot the woman a warning look. She only wished she could compete with Evie, who lacked bleached-blonde hair, fake long nails, and equally fake breasts. Considering the fact that Evie had snagged Damon, the formerly single quarterback, then yeah, he wasn't shocked by the other woman's attitude.

"Since when do you have a girlfriend?" Drew, a tight end, asked.

Damon pulled up one chair next to Emerson, then looked around for another, not finding one.

Evie put her hand on his arm. "Don't worry, honey. We can share."

Evie on his lap again meant a hard-on for the entire night, and he was oddly looking forward to it. He settled into the chair and waited. Evie glanced at him and was about to sit.

"Why don't you take the jacket off?" he asked, wondering not for the first time why she insisted on wearing that thing in the summer, but she seemed attached to it.

She hesitated and shook her head. "I'm fine."

She cuddled into him but she felt stiff and tense, no doubt from the women sitting across from them, trying to keep the attention of Damon's teammates.

He brushed her hair off the back of her neck and whispered in her ear. "Relax. They're jealous they can't compete with how classy you look."

His warm breath hit her neck and she shivered.

He glanced down and noticed her nipples had puckered against her sexy top.

"Classy? Really?" She sounded surprised by his choice of words.

He slid his hand beneath her jacket and cupped her waist. "Classy and sexy," he whispered, pleased with the grin that lifted her plump lips.

"Prescott, you've been hiding her. How long have you been seeing each other?" Emerson asked.

"About a month," Evie said. "But it got serious real fast, didn't it, honey?" She ran her fingers through his hair, obviously back to herself and playing her part.

He'd rather imagine the interaction between them was real.

"It sure did."

She shifted and his body felt like it was on fire. Her thighs aligned with his and her lush breasts pressed against his chest. The fruity scent he associated with Evie penetrated his nostrils and his cock grew hard. He clenched his jaw and attempted to concentrate on what was happening around them.

"So, Damon said you're a quarterback, too? How does that work?" Evie asked, clearly playing dumb, but Emerson didn't know that.

Greg squared his shoulders, pride suffusing his posture. "I'm in now that Damon's out."

A low growl escaped Damon's throat and Evie patted his chest.

"Just for four weeks, Captain," Greg Emerson said, acknowledging Damon's status with the team and his own temporary one.

"Evie, how do you put up with him?" Devon asked with a chuckle.

Evie curled in closer to Damon, her hair brushing his face, and he stifled a groan.

"We're just in sync," she said coyly.

The woman with James rolled her eyes and Damon ignored her. She was a pinup-doll type, perfect for a one and done, but suddenly Damon didn't find her type appealing. At all.

"Are you excited to get to start?" Evie asked Emerson.

The guy glanced at Damon, as if afraid to answer. Like he thought, puppy dog. "It's okay, man. You can admit it. You're thrilled to get the chance to show what you can do."

"Nobody believes you cheated, Captain," Emerson said, deferring to Damon.

James slapped him on the side of the head. "What'd we say when he walked in? Don't bring it up."

His guys had his back, and for that, Damon was grateful. He hoped Evie was getting the same vibe he did from Emerson, because the kid seemed harmless to him.

The rest of the night passed with Evie joking and drinking scotch with the guys, ignoring the jealous women, and asking questions that would give her insight into his teammates.

But Damon had had enough. "Ready to go?" he asked because it was getting late.

"Sure. I just want to go to the ladies' room first." She slid off his lap, and he was glad he could push his chair closer to the table and hide his erection.

He wanted her and had a feeling they were, as she'd said, in sync. But she was clearly independent and understandably wary of men. Which meant he had to ease her into trusting him and ultimately into what she feared most. A relationship. To begin with, somehow he had to get this woman willingly into his bed.

Chapter Five

E vie headed for the ladies' room, doing her best not to stumble in her high heels. She missed her comfortable scuffed boots. She didn't understand why women loved wearing stilettos. Of course, she liked how Damon looked her over when he'd seen her in the short skirt and heels, but she very much preferred being herself. The women's bathroom was the first door, the men's at the end of the hall.

She used the restroom, washed her hands, touched up her lip gloss, and was about to walk out when the woman who'd done the most glaring at her from across the table strode in.

Evie pasted on a fake smile and started forward, eager to get back to Damon and go home.

"You do realize you're not his type," the catty female said.

Evie sighed. "We're really going to do this?"

"I had him first." The woman whose name Evie didn't know placed her hand on her hips and thrust out her breasts.

Evie refrained from rolling her eyes. "How nice

for you. I take it he didn't come back for seconds. I think that tells you plenty."

The woman's face morphed from pleasant to angry in an instant. "He'll get bored of you. Trust me."

Evie smiled. "He hasn't so far. Have a nice night." Holding back the further immature urge to stick out her tongue, she walked out the door, leaving the other woman behind.

She shook her head. Never in a million years would she understand catty women or those who chased after a man who'd used or just didn't want her any more than she understood Damon's past with that type of female. He, like his teammates, could have their pick and took it when they could, and she'd do well to remember that.

Evie stepped into the empty hall and bumped into a hard male body. She wobbled on her heels and immediately reached out to grab on to something or someone before she fell. A strong hand grabbed her elbow, steadying her.

"Oh my God, thank you." She glanced up into eyes she never expected to see. "John!"

Instinct had her reaching for her gun, but the knife at her side that no one could see and the determined gleam in his eye stopped her. "I wouldn't move if I were you."

Unwilling to be his victim again, she struggled to

break his grip as he made his point with his weapon. The sharp blade pricked her skin where her cami top lifted, baring flesh beneath her jacket, and she swallowed hard, memories of the last time he'd used a knife on her vivid in her mind.

"How did you know where I'd be?" she asked.

"That gas leak? I called it in. Then I was able to get into your apartment and plant a listening device," he said, obviously proud of himself. "You can't escape me, Evie."

Forcing the fear away, she asked, "What do you want?"

"For now? I just want you to remember that you ruined my life, and if I can't be happy, neither can you."

Another woman strode out of the restroom, and he pricked her with the point of the blade, warning her not to make a sound. He breathed in her face, making her want to vomit.

"Enjoy your time with your football player because it won't last. I'll make sure of that." He pushed her away, causing her to really stumble as he headed for the exit at the end of the hall.

By the time she righted herself, two men had stepped out of the restroom, blocking her view of his disappearance.

She leaned against the wall, breathing hard, shaking

inside and out.

"Miss? Are you all right?" one of the men asked as he came up to her.

She brought her hand to her side, afraid the nick to her skin was bleeding. "I'm fine. Thank you."

He shrugged and headed back into the bar.

"Evie?" Damon had come around the corner and caught sight of her. "You were gone a long time and Candy, Mandy, whatever her name is came back…" His voice trailed off and he rushed over. "What happened?"

"John was here," she said, hating the tremor in her voice. Her legs shook but she refused to fall apart or be a victim. "He wanted to make his point. With a knife. It seems to be his weapon of choice."

"Son of a bitch. Where is he?" Damon's entire body vibrated with suppressed anger, but she knew it was too late for him to do anything about it.

She tipped her head toward the side exit. "I couldn't get to my gun fast enough. He already had his knife out and got the upper hand. Again."

He exhaled a sharp breath, and she could see the strength it took for him to retrain his focus on her and not the threat, which was gone. For now.

"C'mere." He held out his arms and she gave in, gratefully cuddling in close, absorbing his warmth and the safety he offered.

"He bugged my apartment," she said, glancing up at him.

"What?"

She groaned. "Like I said, one step ahead of me. He used the gas leak as a cover."

Damon frowned. "I'm guessing he was the fire-fighter nobody recognized." Reaching into his pocket, he pulled out his phone. "What's your brother's number?"

Although she had Mack's cell in her contacts, she knew his number by heart and repeated it to Damon.

He dialed and apparently Mack answered quickly because Damon was repeating the incident. "No, don't come here. He's long gone and I don't want a public scene. Evie will stay with me tonight and we can talk tomorrow."

She wasn't about to argue. John hadn't just threatened her, he'd violated her personal space. He'd been in her apartment when she wasn't there, easily blending in with the first responders. She shuddered at the thought.

"Gotta go, Mack. I'll text you my address." He disconnected the call and slid his phone into his back pocket, then met her gaze. "Are you going to give me a hard time about staying over tonight?" he asked, brushing her hair off her face.

She shook her head. "The fact that he found a way

into my apartment and I didn't know it shook me up. I don't like it." And though she wanted to believe she could handle and take care of herself, thus far John had been clever enough not to get caught, but Evie had every intention of having the last laugh.

In the meantime, while she calmed down and pulled herself and some ideas together, she didn't mind going back to Damon's, where she'd feel safe.

*   *   *

Damon rushed Evie out of the bar and back to his car, not bothering to stop by the table on the way out. Holding back his emotions at her being grabbed, threatened, and in some ways violated by her ex wasn't easy, but she needed support, not an explosion of anger on his part. Despite her calm demeanor, he knew she was rattled, and he refused to make it harder on her by showing he was pissed off, too.

He closed her in and climbed into his side of the vehicle. As he drove them home, Evie leaned back against the leather and wriggled her butt into the seat.

"Comfortable?" he asked, grinning at her movements and glad she was managing to relax.

"In these plush seats? You know I am. Although your lap was pretty good, too," she said coyly.

"Be careful how far you push me or I might let you feel how much I liked you there," he warned her, well aware she was deflecting the conversation before he could ask her how she was feeling. But that didn't mean he wouldn't reply honestly. "Do you want to talk about tonight?"

She shook her head, which he caught from the corner of his eye as he drove.

"I'm going to have to go through it again in the morning with Mack. I'd rather not talk about it now." She curled into herself and he regretted asking.

"So, what did you make of the guys at the table tonight?" He changed the charged subject.

She visibly relaxed, leaning against the door. "They're fun. Most of them have no stake in whether you play. In fact, they obviously *want* you in so the team can win. Not that they'd say as much in front of Greg Emerson."

He had the same impression. He gripped the leather steering wheel tighter in his hand.

"I went into meeting him assuming he'd be capable of undermining you. But you're right. He's like a dog that follows you around, doesn't want to piss you off, and at the same time, of course he wants his chance to prove himself." Evie summed up her perception of his backup quarterback with much the same take as Damon had of the guy.

She glanced out at the road as he drove. "I'd never rule out anyone without proof, but my gut says you're right. It's not him."

Damon nodded and turned off his exit. "So, you're okay staying with me tonight?" She hadn't argued when or after he'd said as much to her brother, and Damon hadn't brought up the subject since.

"As long as you know I can take care of myself. I just think it's smarter, knowing that John's found ways into my place I couldn't have foreseen."

He reached out and placed a hand on her arm. "If there's one thing I'm certain of, you're a fighter and you can handle anything that's thrown at you," he said, meaning it.

He pulled into the driveway and parked in his garage, exiting, coming around to help her out, and shutting the door behind her.

She turned, leaning against it. "Thank you for believing in me."

Reaching over, he tucked her hair behind her ear. "There's no saying a woman can't hold her own against a man. You're a private investigator, aren't you?"

She nodded. "And I have to admit it's a fun job sometimes."

"Like when you sat in my lap?" He stepped in close, boxing her in between his body and the car.

She grinned. "It had its moments."

He knew he'd enjoyed it. "Want to know what I

thought about the whole time you were sitting on me?"

She slid her tongue over her lips and he followed the movement, suppressing a groan. "What?"

"This." He leaned forward and pressed his mouth to hers, the taste of her consuming him as he pressed his hard body against her softer one.

She moaned, wrapping her arms around his neck as he slid his hands into her hair and plunged his tongue into her mouth. Eager, too, she reciprocated, her tongue tangling with his, their needs an equal match as desire ramped up between them. Her hips began to grind against his, and he thrust his aching cock into the vee of her hips, over and over again. It was fast and hard and he lost all sense of time and place.

He had no idea how long they stood, making out like horny teenagers, nor did he care until the automatic light in the garage flicked off, leaving them in total darkness.

He stepped back and fumbled for his key fob, finally managing to close the garage door, which reengaged the overhead light.

"We should get inside," he said, his voice gruff. "Straight to my room?" he asked, hoping they were on the same page. If she said no, he'd set her up in the guest room.

He extended his hand and paused, hoping he could take her mind off her ex and give them what they both desired. The choice was hers, and as he waited, his heart pounded in his chest as hard as his cock was inside his pants.

In the near darkness, she slid her palm against his. "Let's go."

*   *   *

Evie knew what she wanted and she desired Damon. She'd be the first to admit she needed a distraction from tonight's events, but that wasn't why she followed Damon into his bedroom. They'd been tiptoeing around their mutual desire for too long.

He used the dimmer and set the lights to low, leading her to the king-size mattress in the middle of the room. "Do you know how long I've been wanting this?"

"Since the day I sat on your lap for the first time?" she asked.

"Nope. Since the first time I laid eyes on you at Dare Nation."

She treated him to a smirk. "When Austin hit you in the head for talking smack."

He laughed at the memory, then began to slide her jacket off, and she stiffened. Somehow she'd forgotten the thing she wanted to hide.

He brushed her hair off her shoulder. "What's up with the jacket?"

"Nothing." Maybe the lights were dim enough he wouldn't notice … and then she wouldn't have to explain.

"Okay, then you don't have to talk about whatever it is. But you can trust me." But he didn't rush to remove the jacket again. "Do you know how sexy you are in black leather?" he asked.

"Yeah?" She forced herself to relax and focus on the hot guy in front of her.

He leaned close and brushed his lips across her neck, causing her body to tremble and her nipples to pucker into tight peaks. "Yeah."

The next time he attempted to slide off her jacket, she allowed the garment to slip off and fall to the floor.

"As much as I love you in leather, I like the view of you in this tank top, too." He dipped his fingers into her cleavage, rubbing the material between his thumb and forefinger, his knuckle brushing her skin. "And I know what I'd like you in even better." His eyes darkened to almost navy. "Absolutely nothing."

Knowing she was fully invested in being with him, she lifted the hem of her shirt and pulled it over her head, baring herself. Her demi-cut bra revealed more than it covered, and based on his low groan, he appreciated her choice.

He reached a hand behind her back and nimbly unhooked the garment, tossing it to the floor with her jacket.

"Impressive move."

He grinned. "That's why they pay me the big bucks."

She laughed and reached for the belt buckle of his jeans, but he took over, making quick work of undressing, while she shed her shoes and jeans, then added her panties to the ever-growing pile of clothing.

She stood up straight and took in his gloriously naked body, her gaze going immediately to his impressive erection. Reaching out, she cupped him in her hand, her fingers barely touching.

With a groan, he pulled away. "I have too much I want to do to you. No rushing me." He lifted her by her waist and settled her on the bed. "Move to the middle of the mattress so I have access to all of you."

Doing as he asked, she scooted to the center, propping herself up on her elbows and watching as he joined her. He prowled toward her, a determined look in his eyes, before leaning down. She expected him to kiss her lips, but he dipped his head and latched on to her nipple, sparking an unexpected tug of desire from her breast to her clit. Arousal like she'd never felt before rushed through her, and she fell back against the mattress.

Closing her eyes, she reached up and grasped on to the headboard, giving him full access, and he took advantage. While one hand cupped and molded her full flesh, his mouth devoured her other breast. He licked and sucked and even bit down on the rigid peak until her hips were arching, her body writhing with need.

He blew on the damp place his mouth had left behind, then switched to her other breast. After giving it the same treatment, his lips trailed down her chest, and ripples of desire added to the arousal already flowing through her. He licked his way over the space between her ribs, down to her belly button, and continued tracing over her lower abdomen.

She sucked in a breath as those talented lips made their way downward. Next thing she knew, that mouth covered her sex and she saw stars. He devoured her like a starving man who'd been given a feast, and she reaped the rewards.

His tongue ran up and down her sex, teasing, tasting, and even nipping along the way. She moaned in delight, grinding herself against his mouth, seeking relief from the building tightness that started low in her body, a growing need that threatened to explode.

His hands came to rest on her thighs, and he sucked her clit into his mouth, torturing her in the best possible way. Her body tingled and sensation mounted until suddenly she flew apart, coming hard, everything inside her coalescing into the most amazing orgasm she'd ever had.

Before she could come back to herself, he'd come over her, his hard cock already covered with a condom, and he began easing himself inside her. Easing being the operative word because he was big and she needed to stretch to accommodate him.

He raised his hips and pushed in deeper. "Okay?"

She grinned. "So damned good. What are you waiting for?"

"That's my sassy girl." He eased out and thrust hard, slamming in until they were joined completely, his hard cock pulsing inside her.

He was big, thick, and she felt him everywhere, and if she'd thought she was a one-orgasm—if she was lucky—girl, she learned differently. She'd been with the wrong men. Because she'd never felt a man like Damon Prescott inside her before.

She also knew he'd ruined her for all other men. And that was before he began to move. A few pumps of his hips and she was climbing toward release again, but before she could gain traction, he pulled out.

"Switch positions," he said, his gaze hot on hers.

She released the headboard, groaning as she lowered her arms because she'd been gripping the iron so tightly.

He helped her up and flipped her onto her belly. "On your knees."

She did as he asked, rising up and glancing over her shoulder. He'd already come over her, his chest pressing to her back, his cock nudging at her entrance. But he paused to seal his lips over hers and kiss her hard before he began thrusting into her, immediately taking her for the ride of her life.

All the pent-up passion they'd been feeling exploded between them. He thrust in and slid back, his hips slamming against her as he picked up rhythm. One arm hooked around her waist, the other tweaking her nipple, he fucked her hard and deep. She moaned and shifted to meet every hit of their bodies together.

Waves of need rose up, emotion running through her, the feeling traveling from her sex through her throat. And when her climax hit, it was sudden and powerful and she needed more.

"Harder, Damon. Please." She drew in a breath at the same time he slammed deep, and she lost track of time and place, every one of her senses gone as Damon owned her, body and soul. But she was keeping her heart. The only person she could trust it with was herself.

* * *

Damon collapsed on top of Evie, realizing immediately he was crushing her. He rolled off, coaxing her into him and inhaling her musky scent as he pulled in deep breaths, coming down from the most intense orgasm he'd ever experienced.

And the sound of her in the throes of pleasure? *Harder, Damon. Please.* He let out a groan. Fuck, but he wanted to hear his name on her lips again and again.

"You okay?" He pressed a kiss to her neck and stayed there, content with a woman for maybe the first time.

"You killed me." The sound she let out was half laugh, half groan.

"It's a talent." He rolled over and she turned, looking into his eyes, realizing immediately he'd said the wrong thing. A bad joke. Evie wasn't just another fuck. She'd never be just another … anything. Not to him. "It's a talent *with you.*"

Something shuttered behind her eyes. A wall of protection he'd seen when he asked about the jacket. Which reminded him of the scar he'd seen when she'd finally stripped for him.

"Come on. We both know you're a playboy when you want to be. And that's fine. We agreed on what this is."

He frowned but she went on.

"I saw how Candy, Mandy, whatever her name was

looked at you. And I'm sure she's not the only one."

He narrowed his gaze, fully aware she had a point. "But there's only one you." She probably thought it was a line. He was deadly serious, but he knew she wasn't ready to hear or believe him.

Before he could watch or listen to her dismiss his honest comment, he rolled off the bed and headed for the bathroom, threw the condom in the trash, cleaned up, and rejoined her, immediately pulling her back into him.

"Hungry?" he asked. They'd only had drinks at the bar and he was starving.

"Sure." She pulled away, seemingly eager to put space between them.

If she'd felt half as much as he had when they were together, she was definitely ducking on him now. He might be a quarterback, throwing a pass his specialty, but Jesse Prescott had drilled every possible play into him and Damon could catch a running target. It might take time, but Evie didn't stand a chance of eluding him in the long run.

"How's pizza sound?" he asked, keeping things light. For now.

"Perfect."

He picked up his cell and, using an app, ordered their food.

While he was taking care of dinner, she pulled on

his tee shirt, grinned, and leaned against the pillows.

"I like you in my clothes." He caught sight of the red scar peeking out from the sleeve of the shirt. Coming to a decision, he ran his hand over the still-angry-colored jagged line. "You can talk to me, you know."

She swallowed hard and remained silent.

"Or not."

She leaned her head back and groaned. "I don't like to talk about it."

He pulled her into him and held her close. "And we can discuss why that is later." Because the emotional issues probably explained much more than how she got the injury. "Let's just start with what happened."

"Okay, fine." She placed a hand on his chest and began playing with the sprinkling of hair there. "It all goes back to John."

"So far all I know is that you had issues and you had to involve the police." He refused to admit he'd looked into the situation in online articles. He was just grateful she was confiding in him now.

She nodded. "Well, we had what I thought was a solid relationship. In fact, we were engaged."

He blinked in surprise. He'd had no idea she had had a fiancé and didn't want to dig into feelings of jealousy now. That went way deeper than he was ready to deal with, and right now he just wanted to understand what made her tick.

"How'd you meet?" he asked when she remained silent.

"I worked for the Miami District Attorney's Office as an investigator. He was a criminal defense attorney at a high-powered firm. Our paths were sure to cross, and when they did, he asked me out."

Sounded normal to him. So far.

He ran a hand up and down her arm, reassuring her, waiting for her to tell him more.

"He worked for a firm with an office in Chicago, and when he had to spend weekends there, it didn't strike me as odd, you know?" She drew in a breath. "And I worked a lot of nights during the week. We still saw each other. Nothing seemed off to me and that's what galls me. I'm supposed to have good instincts when it comes to people and situations!"

"Everyone misjudges someone or something at one time or another," he said, hating how she blamed herself.

She blew out a breath. "Yeah, well. A colleague at the office had a sister who thought her husband was cheating on her. He asked me if I'd look into it. Off the clock." She rolled her shoulders. "He'd done me a solid on a case or two, so I said sure. I asked for the name and information on the husband ... low and behold, it was John Coltrane."

He muttered a curse, pressing a kiss to the top of her head. "I guess there aren't many John Coltranes in Miami?"

"Oh, there were a few. Just one the right age."

Shit. "You told the wife?"

She lifted her head and met his gaze. "I did, at which point I blocked his number on my phone."

"He lost his temper?"

"You could say that. Made a scene at my office, blamed me for ruining his marriage. One of the cops escorted him out. But he was angry and I underestimated him. One night I was coming home from a party for a friend, wearing a dress, my gun was home, my guard was down… He attacked me in an alley. It was surreal." She pushed herself away and held her scarred arm in her hand. "I pressed charges, he lost his job, started to harass me, but he still pulled enough strings to get himself a deal. He blamed me for all of it." She shrugged. "Fast-forward to us going viral and he's back."

"Guy's an ass," Damon muttered, wondering what he could do to get the bastard to back off and leave Evie alone.

The doorbell rang, letting him know the pizza had arrived. "Eat in bed?" he asked.

She answered with a grin.

He walked to the door, deep in thought. He now knew why Evie was so guarded. She'd had her trust betrayed in the worst way and she no longer trusted her judgment. John's return merely reminded her and reinforced her self-doubt.

Damon had every intention of helping her reclaim her belief in herself. It wasn't like he had a game to play, he thought, frustrated. He did, however, have a doctor's appointment tomorrow to get cleared from concussion protocol, which was a start toward coming back. The team physician was someone he met with for cortisone or Toradol shots for his ankle that often gave him trouble—because what athlete didn't need injections to help pain? And now Doc would check his head.

Grabbing the pizza, he stopped by the kitchen for paper plates and napkins, slipped two bottles of water under an arm, and headed back to the bedroom.

A little while later, they were talking about his career and still mulling over how he could have tested positive when he decided to change the subject.

"So why did you leave the DA's office? Actually, why did you become an investigator to begin with?" he asked, taking a bite of his third piece of pizza.

She'd called a halt at two but was drinking from her water bottle. "Dad was a cop. I went to Florida State University, majored in criminal justice." She shrugged. "Everyone in my family serves in one way or another, and though I was fascinated by the system, I had no desire to be a cop and work my way up that ladder."

"You'd be sexy in uniform though." He grinned, causing her to laugh and toss a napkin at him.

"Anyway, I had interned at the DA's office for two summers and met people. One thing led to another, and after graduation, I applied for a job and got it."

"Makes sense. And the reason you left?" He knew he was pushing, but he really wanted to understand her.

A flush rose to her cheeks. "I was embarrassed. Thanks to John's scene there and then his attack, everyone knew I'd been duped. They knew my judgment was suspect. I couldn't face them and I didn't think higher-ups would trust me the way they used to." She glanced down, but she'd put her water on the nightstand, her fingers tracing the scar on her arm. "Becoming a PI was a natural transition. So was working for myself."

He finished his slice and leaned back on the bed, studying her. From her embarrassment to her lack of faith, he thought he understood the leather jacket wearing now, but he needed her to admit the truth.

"Why wear the leather jacket all the time? Because it covers the scar?"

"It's more complicated than that," she murmured.

"Hey. You're looking at someone who understands what it's like to have their word and judgment questioned. You can tell me." He put his hand on hers and pulled it away from her arm.

Lifting her head, she met his gaze. "Because it reminds me that I failed. That my judgment sucks. That I was made a fool of by a man I trusted." Her eyes filled and she pulled her hand back to swipe at the stray tears.

"Hey. You're strong, Evie. From the day I met you, I knew you were tough and could handle anything. Including me." He grinned and she managed a laugh.

"Thank you," she whispered. He could see the gears working and wasn't surprised when she asked, "So where am I sleeping?" And with that, she changed the subject.

"Do you want to go to a guest room?"

She shook her head. "I want to clean up and then I want another round with you."

He could definitely get on board with that.

Chapter Six

Evie slept in, yet she was up before Damon, which was odd, given his normal early schedule. Although she'd risen at eight a.m., they'd been up late last night with what she could only describe as sexual acrobatics. The man was insatiable, and with him, she could claim the same.

She'd woken up in Damon's arms and a panic attack had set in. Not only had she slept with a client, which she could justify because it was her own business but was still unprofessional, she'd slept with a man who got under her skin. Who she was coming to know and *like*.

But she wasn't ready for a relationship, and he'd never denied being happy with his single life and them being a fun fling. Besides, she didn't trust her judgment, especially when it came to men and her personal life. She'd confided in him. She'd trusted him with her deepest fears and insecurities. Though she didn't think he'd use the information to hurt her, it drew her closer to him. And that scared her.

She liked the independent version of Evie Wolfe.

Not the woman who needed a man. Reminding herself they'd agreed to enjoy each other for a while, she calmed down and slipped out from under his arm. He didn't move.

After washing up, she made her way to the kitchen and found his coffee machine, brewing a cup and taking a seat at the granite table. She looked around the brand-new state-of-the-art kitchen. The appliances had foreign names she didn't recognize and the refrigerator was a Sub-Zero, large enough to hold food for an army. Or a big man like Damon, she thought with a grin.

"I like that smile," Damon said in a gruff morning voice.

She glanced up to see him leaning against the doorframe wearing a low-slung pair of sweats and nothing more. She took in his muscular frame from the top of his shoulders down to his bare feet. Even those were sexy.

"Good morning," she said, taking a sip of her coffee, her gaze never leaving his.

"It's a great morning. After an even better night." Striding over, he leaned down and pressed his mouth to hers, parting her lips and tasting her with his tongue, leaving a hint of mint in his wake. She moaned at the delicious invasion.

He lifted his head. "Any idea what time your

brother will be here?" he asked.

She shook her head. "But I can text him." She picked up her phone and sent Mack a message. He answered immediately. "Since we're up, he said he'd come by in an hour."

"Plenty of time then." His slow smile caused flutters in her stomach that only increased when he took her hand and pulled her to her feet.

"What are you doing?"

He grasped her hips and lifted her onto the island in the middle of the kitchen, also granite like the table.

"Ack! It's cold!" She'd pulled on his shirt and it dropped to her knees, but her nearly bare ass was freezing on the granite.

He grinned. "Not to worry. I'm going to warm you up." He eased her back against the stone counter.

Next thing she knew, he hooked his fingers into the sides of her panties and yanked them down and off. He spread her legs, bent down, and licked the seam of her thigh, teasing her with gentle flicks and nips. He held open her sex and pulled her into his mouth, devouring her, sucking and nibbling on her clit.

She arched up her hips, wanting more. The man had a golden talent with his tongue, and she was on the edge almost instantly. When he bit down lightly, she started to come. Gripping the edge of the counter, she writhed back and forth, her hips lifting, grinding against him until she came down from the high to which he'd taken her.

"Holy hell," she muttered, her legs dangling from the granite top.

He lifted her up to a sitting position. "See? You aren't thinking about being cold now, are you?"

"Nope. But I am thinking about this." She slid off the counter and lowered herself to her knees, taking his sweats down next. "I didn't get a chance to taste you yet."

He let out a rough groan and kicked the pants off to the side. She looked at his thick erection and knew this wouldn't be easy. He was a large man, but she wanted to make him feel good. And she really wanted to see her effect on him.

She reached out and gripped him, running her hand over the velvety steel of his cock, using the pre-come on the tip to lubricate her palm.

"Harder," he said in a gruff tone.

Happy to accommodate him, she grasped him tighter and pulled back and forth, tugging on his hard flesh until he was thrusting into her hand. Only then did she release her clasp and guide him into her open mouth.

As she closed her lips around as much of him as she could take, he shuddered, his fingers coming to rest on her head.

"Fuck. You feel so good. Warm and wet." He jerked his hips forward, and she relaxed her mouth, letting him slide in deeper, doing her best to handle him.

She rested her hands on his thighs, and he began to move, gliding out and in, picking up a rhythm yet stopping short of hitting the back of her throat. She sucked, her lips surrounding his thick erection, and he groaned, his hips moving faster until he let go, spurting in her mouth, his entire body trembling as he came.

She released him to catch her breath but she was very pleased at how fast she'd made him climax and how hard he'd orgasmed.

Looking up at him, she grinned. "Good?"

"The best."

He helped her to her feet and pulled her close for a deep, warm kiss that pushed past all those boundaries she'd tried to put back after walking out of his bedroom this morning.

Then, as if he woke up with her in his bed and kitchen every morning, he strode over to make himself a cup of coffee.

Her gaze fell to his broad back and she sighed. He was easy to like. To have fun with. And she could fall for him so effortlessly, but she needed to remind herself that's all this was.

Fun and short-term.

*　*　*

Damon dressed, then leaned against the armoire in the bedroom and groaned, listening to the blow dryer in the bathroom. He'd convinced Evie to share a shower that was *just a shower* before her brother arrived. No sex had been involved, but he'd never look at soap and not think of the way she'd leaned over and lathered her legs, her stomach, and her breasts again.

All the while, a wicked smile had curved her lips. Lips that had just recently been wrapped around his cock.

Evie strode out of the bathroom wearing a pair of sweats his sister kept in a guest room for when she stayed over and one of Damon's tee shirts because he'd liked how she looked wearing his clothes.

Seeing his shirt wrapped around her curves had him feeling possessive, the need to hold her, keep her safe, and make her his overwhelming. But it was way too soon to even broach the idea of a long-term relationship, especially given that she was still dealing with her past and was far from ready to consider a future with him.

He couldn't believe his mind had gone there already, but Evie brought something unexpected to his life. The urge to protect someone who wasn't family. The emotions that had built in his chest when he'd come deep inside her body were foreign but clearly meaningful. As was the desire to just be with her and enjoy her company. That she'd trusted him with her deepest fear and pain had been humbling. And he wanted to build on that trust.

"Ready to deal with my brother?" she asked.

"Definitely." He wanted a solution to the loose cannon that was John, lurking in the shadows and threatening Evie.

As they headed downstairs, the doorbell rang.

He let Mack inside and the man immediately pulled his sister into an embrace. "Jesus. If you weren't with Damon, I would have come right away."

She hugged him back. "I know. And I'm okay."

He released her and Damon led them to the family room, his favorite room in his house. The huge leather couch with recliners on either end had been a find. Of course, he'd hung a large-screen television on the wall, and his mother had discovered a unique rock formation table to sit in front of the sofa. One that could withstand Damon and his brothers propping their feet on, which, after encouraging Evie to sit, Damon did.

"I'm going to kill the bastard," Mack said, pacing back and forth in front of the table, his agitation clearly preventing him from sitting down.

"I want him off the streets," Evie said. "He can't go around threatening me with a knife." She shuddered at the memory, and Damon pulled her into him, a move not missed by her eagle-eyed brother, who narrowed his gaze.

Damon shot him a level stare, shrugged, and kept his arm around Evie, making his point. He was here to stay. In case he hadn't been clear enough the other day.

Mac inclined his head. "Well, I did some digging. John's unemployed. Can't get a job with his record, which is probably why he's so pissed at you. I'm sure he could have found you before now, but seeing you hanging with the star of the Miami Thunder clearly set him off."

"Clearly," Evie muttered.

"I think he's spiraling and I want to find him. I have an APB out on him. Don't worry. He'll turn up," Mack said by way of reassurance. But from the tight set of his shoulders, Damon wasn't certain Mack knew where to find the SOB.

Evie shifted against him. "I should talk to his ex-wife. Maybe she's heard from him."

"No!" Damon and Mack shouted at once.

She shoved herself away from Damon and glared at both men. "Seriously?"

Damon squeezed her hand. "I have no doubt

you're capable of talking to her. I just don't want to give John any more reason to go after you."

Mack nodded in agreement. "And I don't want you exposed, going to a place where John might actually show up."

"I keep saying I can handle myself and he keeps making me look inept. I hate it." She jumped out of her seat, agitated and upset.

Damon met Mack's gaze. He was concerned about Evie, worried she'd do something to find John that was impulsive, just to prove she was capable.

"Stop with the looks, will you? I'm right here. I can make my own decisions and I'm also not stupid. I'll call his ex. I still have her number." With that, she stormed out of the room.

Mack shook his head, staring after her. "She's always been stubborn and independent."

"With four older brothers and a cop for a father, I imagine she felt the need to prove herself more often than not," Damon said.

"Never thought of it like that."

Damon rose to his feet. "Want a drink?" he asked the other man. "Soda? Water? Beer?"

"On duty and I need to get going. Look, she's going to want to handle things herself. I need you to watch out for her," Mack said, just as Evie walked back into the room and glared at her brother.

"Talking for me again? First, Amanda, John's ex-wife, hasn't seen or heard from him, but she promised to call if she does. Second, did you forget what I do for a living? I sure as hell will be more careful now."

"I can't just turn off worrying about you," Mack said. "Are you going to stay here until we find him? Because your apartment is open with the catwalk, close to the elevator, and leaves you vulnerable."

Damon had every intention of keeping Evie at his house, but he knew better than to say so.

She glanced up at him. "Do you mind? It is smarter."

"Wouldn't have it any other way." Damon winked at her.

Blushing, which he found sexy, she turned to her brother. "Can you talk to the bar owner? See if they have a camera in that back hall? Maybe we can get a tape of him threatening me with the knife."

Damon was impressed with her ingenuity.

"You got it," Mack said. "Now I'm going to do my job. Keep in touch and I'll do the same." He reached an arm out, pulled Evie to him, and kissed her forehead. "You know I'm just worried about you."

She inclined her head. "And I appreciate it. But I'm sick of feeling impotent thanks to John and frustrated that you think my movements should be dictated by the whims of a psycho."

"Love you, Evie."

Mack obviously knew better than to get into another argument. Together, Damon and Evie walked him to the door.

Once he was gone, she turned to him. "What's on your agenda for today?"

"Doctor's appointment for my head. I can at least get cleared even if I can't play."

"Team doctor? One you see often?" she asked.

He nodded.

"Then I'm coming with you. In case you forgot, we're still working on your case, too."

"Great." This way he could keep an eye on her. He was just too smart to mention it.

*　　*　　*

Evie and Damon stopped at her apartment for her to switch into an outfit of her own, then pack up clothing and personal items to bring back to his house. Her brothers had stopped by, and Mack had found the bug John planted, disposing of it for her. She still didn't feel perfectly safe here, but at least she wasn't being watched. She changed into a pair of jeans and a tank top. Her leather jacket lay on her bed, and out of habit, she reached for it and paused.

She wore the jacket to protect herself from the memories and insecurities that arose every time she saw the scar. Not to mention she hadn't wanted Damon to notice. But he'd already seen her pain and questioned her about her past. And she'd been forced to talk about it. Face it. So, the question arose. Did she continue to hide herself? Or did she begin the slow process of acceptance and healing? Jacket or no jacket, it wasn't like she could forget, not with John lurking around.

She left the garment on the bed and continued to pack before ending up back in Damon's car, her mind going to her brother's overprotectiveness. She didn't want to be angry with Mack for wanting to keep her safe, but he was questioning her ability, the very thing she'd left her job at the DA's office to avoid happening. And he'd done it in front of Damon, who'd all but backed her brother up. But they were both just concerned.

"Hey. Are you okay?" Damon put a hand on her knee before placing it back on the wheel.

She shrugged. "Frustrated." She didn't elaborate, not wanting to get into it again.

Before he could reply, his cell phone rang. It was connected to the car, and Austin's name came up on the screen. He hit a button. "Hey."

"Hey. Can you talk?" Austin asked.

"Sure. Evie's in the car with me."

"Even better. I was planning on calling her next."

Damon glanced over and she raised her eyebrows in question.

He pulled into the doctor's office lot and parked. "Okay, what do you need to tell us?"

Austin cleared his throat. "Can you guys come to the office this afternoon at three? I have a surprise for Quinn, and I want the people we care about to be there."

Evie let out an excited squeal. "Oh my God, you're asking her to marry you!"

"Dude!"

Austin chuckled. "I know it's last-minute, but it's all planned. I just decided to have family and friends there. Are you guys free?"

Evie could hear the excitement in his brother's voice.

"If I wasn't, I'd make myself free," Damon said. "But yeah, we're fine and of course we'll be there."

Evie was practically bouncing with joy in her seat at the news.

Damon disconnected the call, glanced at her, and grinned. "Happy?"

"I'm thrilled for my best friend. I never thought I'd see the day she married a man with a baby. Her own ready-made family. This from the woman who said no kids." Evie shook her head. "Just shows you that you never know what life has in store."

Meeting her gaze, he treated her to a slow smile that had her stomach twisting with need and seemed to carry a hidden message. One she wasn't ready to decipher or know.

* * *

Damon walked into the team doctor's office outside of the stadium, Evie by his side, his stomach in knots. Although the doctor's decision didn't mean he'd be allowed to play in the first four games, it would be an important step toward returning both to the team and to his exercise and readiness routine. And those would keep him in shape and get him ready to play as soon as he could return.

The receptionist checked him in, and soon after, the nurse, Lana, opened the door to the treatment rooms. "Damon? We're ready for you."

He rose to his feet and gestured for Evie to join him. If he was going to get to the bottom of his issues, he wanted and needed her by his side.

She stood, following him inside. Once in the patient room indicated by Lana, he sat on the exam table and Evie took the chair against the wall, watching him intently. She had a calming influence on him, his rapidly beating heart slowing just because he could look over and see her there.

And when she smiled, he was able to return it.

Two raps sounded at the door, and when it opened, Dr. Jonas walked in, clipboard in hand. As usual, he wore a white jacket over his clothes and a stethoscope around his neck. He looked around the same age as Damon's uncle Paul, with a head of salt-and-pepper hair and a kind look in his eyes. Always.

"Damon! Good to see you."

"Wish I could say the same," Damon said wryly. He'd prefer not to have to deal with a concussion on top of a suspension.

Doc chuckled. "I understand." He turned to Evie. "And who is this?" he asked, extending his arm.

"Evie Wolfe," she said, and before Damon could introduce her, she rose to her feet and shook his hand.

"Nice to meet you, Ms. Wolfe," he said with a curious expression on his face.

Damon glanced at Evie. "Evie's my … girlfriend." He played the ruse because it was necessary, and Evie seemed to smile and go along.

The older man looked surprised. No doubt because Damon never had a long-term girlfriend, no woman he'd labeled as such, and none he'd ever have brought with him to an important appointment like this one.

"Well, I'll be damned," Doc said, grinning at Evie. "A miracle happened."

Doc had been with the team so long, blurting

things out was second nature, and now he'd just helped cement Evie's belief that Damon didn't do relationships.

"How's the head?" Doc asked, putting his items on the countertop, then turning to Damon.

He shrugged. "Fine, Doc."

"Dizziness?"

Damon shook his head. "Nope. Once it went away, it never came back."

"Ears?"

"No ringing."

Doc slapped his shoulder. "Good. Now let's check you out." Over the course of the next half hour, he ran a series of neurological exams that included cognitive and balance tests before turning to the computer that hung in the room and pulling up Damon's chart.

"So. Looks like you're back to your baseline," Doc said.

Damon glanced at Evie. "Every player takes these tests early in the season so Doc here has a baseline of comparison. He knows what he expects to see if he's going to clear me to come back."

She nodded in understanding. "Makes sense."

He was surprised she hadn't asked any questions yet, but knowing Evie, they would come.

"Let's go talk in my office," Doc said.

Damon's hand on Evie's back, they followed Doc

out the door to the end of the hall and entered the man's domain. He had wooden bookshelves behind his desk and an array of team memorabilia on the shelves.

He settled behind his desk and picked up a pen, rotating it between his palms. "Okay, Damon. I'm going to clear you for light aerobic exercise with Jimmy. Once he sees that's no problem, you can move to step three. Continued aerobic exercise and strength training. You know the drill for return to participation protocol. After that, we can get you into full football activity and clear you. Unfortunately, you can't play for the next four games. Five weeks pretty much. I'm sorry."

Damon's gut churned at the reminder.

"Doctor, do you have any theories on how Damon tested positive for performance-enhancing drugs considering he hasn't taken any?" Evie asked, perking up now that Doc had reached his conclusion.

The man glanced at Evie, eyes narrowing at her question. It wasn't every day an NFL player let a woman ask questions about his treatment, that much Damon knew. Unless it was his wife.

Still, Evie had a job to do, and Damon had every intention of letting her do it. He nodded at Doc, encouraging the man to answer.

"It's as much a mystery to me as it is to Damon.

We've spoken about it and I don't know. There has to be something in a supplement or medication he ingested that he doesn't remember." Doc picked up his clipboard. "Still an old-fashioned kind of guy. Don't trust computers completely," he joked as he made some notes.

Evie didn't reply.

Damon glanced at her and she had her gaze on the diplomas on the wall.

"I see you graduated from Duke University and stayed for med school. Did you like North Carolina?" she asked.

His expression grew perplexed, obviously confused by her topic of conversation.

So was Damon.

"Good weather, great football and basketball at Duke. No complaints. Have you been there?" he asked.

She shook her head. "But I've heard great things."

"You'd enjoy it. Maybe you could get Damon here to take you on a visit."

"Maybe," she murmured. "Did you keep in touch with a lot of people from your college or med school days? I know I'm still best friends with my room-mate."

Doc gave her an amused glance. "I suppose. Some I lost touch with. Others pop up now and again."

Still perplexed by her conversation, he glanced at Doc. "All set?" He was ready to get out of here.

"I just wanted to ask about your ankle. You're due for an injection. Unless you want to put it off until right before you return to play?" Doc was already reaching for the cabinet where he kept the small bottles of medicine.

But Damon wasn't putting another damn thing in his body right now. Not even the usual. "I'll wait."

Doc shrugged and closed the door. "No problem. Your choice."

"What's wrong with your ankle? What kind of injection?" Evie asked, concern etching her pretty features.

Damon tipped his head. "Go ahead, Doc. I'll talk to her."

He nodded. "Good to meet you, Evie. Damon, take care. Call me if you need anything." Doc picked up his trusty clipboard and walked out, shutting the door behind them.

Evie popped up from her chair. "What's going on? You never mentioned shots when we talked."

"I forgot about them, to tell you the truth. They're part of my routine." It wasn't any different than taking ibuprofen for pain. He rolled his shoulders. "Ask any pro player and you'll find out they're getting injections of something on one body part or another. Toradol,

Marcaine. As long as we can play, we do it."

She narrowed her gaze. "Huh. Okay," she said, but she didn't seem satisfied with his answer.

"What about you? Why all the questions about Duke and North Carolina?"

"I'll tell you in the car." And on that note, they headed out of the office and on to their next stop.

Dare Nation.

*   *   *

As Evie sat in the passenger seat of Damon's car, she should be excited for her best friend, who was about to have a surprise proposal. Instead her head was spinning. First there was Doc, who'd been utterly shocked to see a woman by Damon's side, which made sense. For one thing, she was sure any player bringing a woman to a doctor's appointment was rare. But in Damon's case, Doc had confirmed her notion that Damon Prescott was a player. She was just the convenient woman in his bed.

She couldn't deny that Damon was being a great friend, taking her in, honestly worrying about her. But that's all he was. A friend with benefits. Her stomach twisted but she told herself it was fine. That's all she wanted from him anyway. No matter how easy it was to fall for him.

Clearing her throat, she forced her mind back to

Damon's case and the information she'd come up with at Doc's. From the minute she'd laid eyes on Dr. Jonas's diplomas on the wall, she'd made the connection. She just didn't know if Damon would want to hear it. Whether he'd believe it or think it was just coincidence. She was trying to figure it out herself.

"Hey. Are you going to tell me about North Carolina?" Damon, one hand on the steering wheel, turned toward her for a second and asked.

"I'm going to put out a scenario, and I want you to keep an open mind." She shifted in her seat and tucked a leg beneath her.

He nodded. "Go ahead. I'm listening."

"Okay, I did some research into your backup quarterback. Did you know his father is a doctor?"

"Nope. It's not like we sit around and talk about our parents in the locker room." He shot her a curious look. "So … what's this about?"

She bit down on the inside of her cheek. "His father is Dr. Lyle Emerson, the Chair of Duke University School of Medicine. He's a pediatric oncologist. His mom's an investment banker at Circle One Investments. Obviously in North Carolina. His father graduated from Duke."

Silence surrounded them in the car as she waited for him to make the connection.

"You think Emerson's parents have something to

do with Doc dosing me with an illegal substance?" His knuckles turned white as he gripped the steering wheel.

"I think it's something to consider," she said carefully.

He shook his head. "The man's been treating me since day one. He's like a father to us when we're injured." His voice rose defensively.

"Relax. I'm just pointing out the possibility. I haven't made an official connection yet." But she planned to dig deeper and find out.

Knowing she'd pushed enough and he wouldn't want to hear supposition, she turned her focus to their afternoon. "In the meantime, can we go home so I can change? My best friend and your brother are about to get engaged."

Chapter Seven

E vie and Damon walked into Dare Nation, where they were greeted by the receptionist, Hannah, who Evie had come to know in the last year Quinn had been working there. Evie and Quinn often met for lunch, and because Evie made her own hours, she often came by Dare Nation to pick up her friend.

"Hi, Hannah."

"Hey, Hannah," Damon said.

"How are you?" the pretty brunette asked.

Evie smiled. "Hanging in there. Busy. You?"

"Same. I'm excited," she whispered. "Mr. Prescott is having everyone gather in the conference room." She glanced toward Quinn and Austin's office and gestured for Evie and Damon to follow her the other way.

They ducked into the large room and Evie blinked. The space was filled with red roses. They lined every counter space, the table, and the pedestals in the corners.

She couldn't stop the smile that spread across her face, happiness for her best friend filling her. Across the room, she caught sight of Paul Dare and some other agents, along with clients she knew Quinn was fond of and Damon's sister, Bri.

Damon strode toward them, and as she watched him go, her heart skipped a beat. All morning she'd been in PI mode, doing her best to pay attention to the doctor and his demeanor and put what was going on between her and Damon out of her mind. Except now, in a more personal setting, she couldn't take her eyes off him.

He was handsome in a pair of black jeans that hugged his thighs and a white tee shirt that accentuated his bulging muscles. Although her gaze was on his ass at the moment, he hadn't shaved today, and the scruff on his face added to his sex appeal.

She sighed in delight and headed over to make small talk with someone she knew. The longer she mingled, the more crowded the room grew. Apparently Austin had invited their immediate world. And it was sweet.

She picked up a glass of champagne from the drinks on the corner of a credenza and took a sip of the bubbly. "Mmm." She smiled at the delicious taste.

"Someone looks happy … and, in case I didn't mention it earlier, gorgeous." His hot gaze skimmed over her tight wrap blouse with a slight teasing V and black leggings that tied at the ankles, her red stilettos completing the outfit.

Knowing she was going to be seeing people in Damon's industry, she'd dressed up to play his girl-friend. But a part of her couldn't help but wonder, when the job was over, if he would still like her as the real Evie. Not that he'd complained when she'd gone to the doctor in jeans and a tank, but sometimes with these people she felt out of her element. Though she really did like this outfit even if she did save it for undercover-type work.

He cupped her face in his hands, leaned close, and slid his lips over hers, making her forget everything but him. She gasped in surprise, but when he nipped on her lower lip, she melted into him and kissed him back, a tongue-tangling duel that had her head spin-ning and desire ramping her up.

"Ahem. Am I interrupting?" a male voice asked.

Evie gasped and jerked back, but Damon kept ahold of her, his arm around her waist. She'd forgotten they were in public.

"Uncle Paul." Damon grinned.

"So, is this for show?" he asked in a low voice. "Or is it real? Because it looked pretty authentic to me." He chuckled, low and deep.

"It looked that way to me, too," Paul's partner, Ron Mayburn, said, also keeping his voice down. He obviously understood the necessary discretion in their circumstances.

She swallowed hard, unsure of what Damon would say. They'd agreed to enjoy each other for now, but that wasn't something she'd admit in public.

"We're showing people what they need to see," Damon said, but he pulled her close to him.

Her throat filled and she couldn't swallow, because a part of her wished it could be real, but she also had just been put in her place. Which was good, because as she understood, not only were they from two different worlds, she just couldn't imagine herself taking that leap of faith in a man again. Once Damon returned to playing football full-time, he wouldn't have time for her, anyway.

"It looks like everyone's here," Paul said, interrupting her thoughts.

Evie glanced around and waved at Quinn's family, who congregated in a corner.

"Wow. Austin really wanted an audience," Damon said, chuckling.

"I think he wants to prove to her this is it for him," Paul explained.

Damon nodded. "My brother never expected to get married, let alone have a baby. Now he's got a family and I've never seen him happier. He wants to nail it down."

"We'll catch up with you later," Paul said, walking

away with Ron just as an unfamiliar voice spoke.

"Damon."

He stiffened, keeping Evie hugged close to his side. "Ian. Good to see you."

Recognizing the name, she realized this was his cousin and team owner, and she imagined Damon wasn't thrilled to face him at the moment.

But Damon remained calm. "Ian, this is Evie Wolfe. Evie, my cousin and the Miami Thunder team owner, Ian Dare."

"It's a pleasure," Ian said, shaking Evie's hand, but he looked at Damon grimly. "Any news?"

Evie glanced at him, wondering if he'd mention the connection between the team doctor and trainer.

"We're working on it," was all Damon said.

Before Ian could press him more, the conference room door opened and Austin stepped inside, his baby daughter in his arms and an obviously confused Quinn by his side.

"What is this?" she asked, taking everyone in. "The people, the roses…?"

"The ring," Austin said. "I decided since we didn't get together in a traditional way, my proposal wasn't going to be traditional, either."

"Proposal?" Quinn squeaked out. "Now?"

Evie grinned at her friend's shock.

"I thought it was important to have our friends

and family around us for this moment," he said.

As Austin reached into his pocket, Damon pulled Evie tighter against him. Instead of fighting it, she leaned into his solid warmth.

Austin held out a ring box. One look and even Evie recognized the red and gold Cartier logo and color.

Quinn gasped and covered her mouth with her hand, happy tears in her eyes.

He handed the baby to Hannah, then got down on one knee. "Quinn, before you, I was alone, lonely, and I hadn't given the idea of family a thought. Before us"—he glanced at the baby his assistant bounced on her hip—"you thought you didn't want one."

He grinned. "But then this little munchkin came and brought us together … when we really belonged with each other all along. Quinnlyn Stone, will you marry me? And adopt Jenny because you're the only mother she'll ever know?"

Quinn's eyes bright, cheeks flushed, her smile wide, Quinn said, "Yes. Yes, of course I will."

Austin slid the ring on her finger and then she was in his arms, Jenny scooped up and cuddled between them.

Evie sniffed, watching as Quinn's big family surrounded her, followed by the office staff.

Evie waited, knowing she'd have time with her

best friend later.

"Who knew you were a softie," Damon said beside her.

She glanced up at him. "There's a lot you don't know about me, Prescott."

He grinned. "Then I look forward to peeling back more layers and finding out what else lies beneath." At his double entendre, her nipples puckered and her panties grew damp.

She wanted him, and in this, at least, they were on the same page. He was going through a life crisis. She was dealing with the return of her stalker ex and she didn't trust her judgment with men, especially this handsome, famous playboy football player. But they both yearned for an escape from reality, and she couldn't deny how much she wanted to find hers in Damon's arms.

* * *

The engagement party had been more difficult than Damon had thought it would be. Pretending to be together with Evie when he wanted a relationship in reality was wearing on him, but he was certain he was handling her right. Getting her to a place where she could finally realize she could put her fears behind her and trust him was the only way to go. If he sprung his growing feelings on her now? Well, she'd run and that would put her in more danger with her stalker ex.

But when it came to desire? On that they were in agreement. He saw the heat in Evie's eyes. It matched the fever running through his veins. Despite the fact that they'd had a long night and morning of hot sex, he wanted her again now. Hard and hot, his cock cocooned in her damp heat.

As much as he wanted to take her home now, she had a job to do. More research on Doc and Emerson's father first. Much to Damon's relief, Ian had taken off after congratulating the happy couple, enabling Damon to relax. He had no desire to face his cousin or the disappointment in his eyes again. It didn't matter how much Damon proclaimed his innocence, right now the failed test spoke louder than his words.

First up, though, the congratulations. While Evie finally got her time with Quinn, Damon made his way to his brother and pulled him into a hug. The rest of the family had already given him their best—his mom, Bri, and Jaxon. Only Braden, still abroad with Doctors Without Borders, was missing. He made a mental note to try and get through to his sibling soon.

"I'm happy for you, Austin. You deserve the best." He slapped his brother on the back. "Quinn is perfect for you." He glanced at the woman now holding Jenny and grinning as she spoke to her best friend.

"Your time will come," Austin said, not subtly

glancing at Evie. "I saw that kiss," he said, his voice low. "I get keeping up appearances but don't hurt her. Don't put me in the middle of you and Quinn."

Damon scowled. If either of them was going to get hurt, he had a hunch it would be him. Still, he resented his brother's implication. "Don't think so little of me," he muttered. "I know how to treat a lady."

"Not from what I've seen up until this point."

Damon held up his hands. "Fine. Fair. But none of them were Evie."

Austin's eyes opened wide. "It's serious between you?"

"It is for me. For her? I've convinced her we're having fun for now. It's the only way I could start to make inroads." But Evie was worth the work and the effort. He shoved his hands into his front pockets. "I'm trying to show her we can work."

A slow grin lifted his brother's lips. "Well, I'll be damned."

"Damon!" His mother, Christine, called his name, and Damon turned as Austin faced another well-wisher.

"Mom!" He gave her a kiss on the cheek. "You look wonderful." Wearing a simple patterned dress, her blondish-brown hair resting on her shoulders, his mother was beautiful as always.

"How's my baby boy?" She patted his cheek and

he groaned.

"Not a baby."

"Okay, sorry. You're all my babies. But seriously. How are you?" she asked with an amused smile.

He swallowed hard. "It's rough," he admitted to one of the few people he'd be truthful with. "I didn't do it. The world thinks I did. My teammates think I let them down. I don't know how Emerson will play and I'm sick over it all."

She placed a hand on his cheek. "Listen to me, Damon Prescott. You are a strong man. You survived your tough father and you'll get through this."

"Mom—"

She shook her head. "I never said anything and I know this isn't the place, but I'm sorry. Sorry I stayed. Sorry I thought I could temper his personality with you boys."

"Don't go there. It's in the past."

"But it made you tough, and because of that, I know you'll handle this." She managed a smile. "That said, I also notice you aren't doing it alone. Who's the woman I saw you kissing, hmm?"

"Yeah, Damon. Who did we see you kissing?" His brother, Jaxon, put one hand on their mother's shoulder and another on Damon's.

"Go away," he jokingly said to his brother.

"No can do. I'm in town so here I am. Well? Who

is she?"

Deciding he might as well introduce everyone, Damon gestured for Evie to come join them. She walked over, that long hair hanging over her shoulders, her brown eyes wide with curiosity.

"Evie Wolfe, I'd like you to meet my mother, Christine, and this moron is my brother, Jaxon. Mom, Jax, my … girlfriend, Evie."

While everyone, including Evie, digested that introduction, Damon merely grinned. Sure, Evie probably thought his declaration was for show as they'd agreed while she investigated, but Damon knew it was fucking real. Otherwise he'd never introduce her to his mother as his girlfriend. He'd have fudged the wording and explained later. At least he didn't feel like he was lying to his mother. Not on his end, anyway.

"Oh my goodness. It's nice to meet you!" His mom pulled a shocked Evie into a hug.

"It's a pleasure to meet you, too, Mrs. Prescott. Jaxon." Evie smiled at them, but Damon knew she wasn't sure of herself. Which was fine. He had enough confidence for them both.

His mom frowned. "None of that Mrs. Prescott stuff. Call me Christine."

"Hi, Evie. What do you see in my jerk of a brother?" Jaxon grinned. "I'm kidding. Damon has great taste."

Evie blushed and Damon pulled her into a hug.

"And I can't wait to get my girl alone. Dinner next time you're in town?" Damon asked his brother. "Lord knows I have the time." His stomach churned at the reason.

"You'd better believe it." Jax stared at him, and Damon knew it was because he couldn't believe his one-and-done brother had found and claimed a woman.

"I'll call," Damon promised.

Christine glanced at Evie. "I'd love to have lunch and get to know you better."

"Oh. I…"

"I'll give her your number," Damon said, relieving Evie before she stuttered over her answer. "Listen, guys, I want to say goodbye to Austin and Quinn and get going. Talk to you both soon."

"It was nice to meet you," Evie said.

"Call me," his mother reminded her. "Or I'll get your number from Damon and call you."

He grinned. Christine Prescott was persistent. Like it or not, Evie was in for a nice prying lunch with his mother.

After extricating themselves, he grasped Evie's hand, and they made their way back to Austin and Quinn. "Welcome to the family," he said, giving her a hug.

"Thanks, Damon."

"How are you doing?" Quinn asked, looking at him with concern in her eyes.

He forced a smile at the unspoken reason for the question. "I'm okay. Really." He didn't want anything ruining her day.

After a few more minutes, someone pulled Quinn away.

Damon turned to Evie. "Ready to go?"

"More than ready. Who knew meeting all these people was going to be ridiculously exhausting?"

He took her hand. "Then let's go home."

As they approached the car, with the sun shining overhead and Evie looking gorgeous, he turned and pulled out his phone. "Let's take a picture," he said with a grin.

She stopped and met his gaze. "What? Why?"

He laughed, knowing this was a complete role reversal. Damon Prescott taking a selfie. It was enough to make him gag. "We need to make us Instagram official."

Her eyes opened wide. "But we aren't a couple!"

"We are in the eyes of everyone in my world, aren't we?" And the deeper he could embed her in his life, the harder it would be for her to dig her way out.

"Won't this piss off John? Push him into doing something else?"

He'd considered that. "Or maybe it'll force him to come out of hiding. And make a mistake."

With a shrug, she came to his side. He wrapped one arm around her, held up the camera with the other, and snapped the perfect shot.

Then he took the time to upload to social media.

*   *   *

Meeting Damon's family. Being invited to lunch by Damon's mother. Damon taking a selfie to make them Instagram official. What world had Evie landed in? This was all more than she'd anticipated when she'd agreed to this charade, and she was exhausted.

"You okay?" Damon asked as he pulled the car into the driveway.

Oh. Maybe she should add to her bizarre list getting used to riding in a two-hundred-and-fifty-thousand-dollar vehicle. She glanced at her slacks, bought on sale at Marshalls, the blouse she'd found at Target and sighed.

The sound of a car horn had her jumping in her seat.

Damon turned and let out a whoop, turned the vehicle off, and practically flew out the door. Evie climbed out in time to see him engulfed by three large men, their laughter and joy in seeing each other obvious.

She walked over and waited for the back slapping and brother-like hugging to end.

Finally, Damon stepped back and caught her gaze, gesturing for her. "Evie, come meet the guys!"

She looked up and into the startling blue stare of Harrison Dare, A-list actor, action movie hero, and eye candy for most women in America. With his jet-black hair and muscled body, he had presence most other guys would envy.

"Hi … I … I'm—" She stuttered like any normal woman would.

"Evie, I take it you recognize Harrison Dare. Am I going to have to beat up my cousin?"

Harrison laughed, dimples framing his mouth. "Nice to meet you, Evie."

"Nice to meet you, too," she managed.

"I'm Nick," another good-looking, dark-haired man said.

Evie shook his hand.

"And this bozo is Asher," Damon, looking more relaxed than she'd ever seen him, said with a smile.

Asher, also gorgeous, grinned and, without warning, pulled her into a hug. "Hey, pretty lady." He released her. "Are you why Damon's been ducking my calls? He's too busy with a new girlfriend?" He looked her over in what she'd call a respectful way. "I wouldn't blame him."

Evie felt a blush rise to her cheeks. "He's got enough on his plate without worrying about romance, wouldn't you say?"

"That's why we're here." Asher, who had darker hair, hooked an arm around Damon's neck. "We're going to take his mind off his problems. Zach and Emery are sorry they couldn't make it, by the way."

"It's all good."

Damon ushered them into the house, handed out drinks, and soon they were sitting around the family room. The guys had beers, and Evie, still wiped out after the day she'd had, just kicked back in one of the recliner chairs at the end of the couch.

"How's your head?" Asher asked Damon. "And don't fucking lie to me."

"I got the green light to start light workouts this morning." Damon took a pull of his beer.

Asher glanced at Evie. "He's okay?"

She nodded. "He is."

Damon scowled. "Since when isn't my word good enough?" he muttered.

"Evie, what's your story?" Asher cocked his head to the side, those golden eyes focused on her.

She shrugged. "I'm—" She glanced at Damon for permission to tell the truth and he nodded.

"I'm a private investigator. I'm looking into who could have slipped Damon performance-enhancing drugs and caused him to test positive," she admitted.

Harrison frowned. "Fucking sucks, man."

"So that means you guys aren't a real couple?" Asher asked.

"We're together for now," Evie said before he could answer.

Asher glanced between them. "Okay." He grinned, then tipped back his beer bottle and took a sip. "You're staying here, though?" He looked at Evie. "I mean, you two changed into more casual clothes upstairs." Asher pressed her for answers. He seemed the closest to Damon, the most invested in his life.

"I'm having some issues Damon's helping me with." She had no intention of getting into her personal life and admitting her vulnerabilities.

She glanced at Nick. Obviously the quietest one, he channel surfed while they talked.

"So, Evie. Did Damon ever tell you about the time he came out to Hollywood and he was a walk-on in one of my movies?" Harrison asked.

"Get out of here." She leaned forward in her seat, crossing her legs.

"Deadly serious."

"Tell me more." She rested her chin on her hands, focused on the man who knew how to command attention even in a room full of other hot men, one of whom Evie couldn't get out of her head.

Damon took a swig of beer. "Can we not go there?"

Harrison grinned. "He told his family and friends he had a walk-on. Got everyone together to watch. But when the director did his thing, all you could see on-screen was the back of Damon's head." He, the other two men, and even Evie burst out laughing.

"I can only imagine the shit your family gave you," she said.

The men continued to tell old stories, kid pranks to adult brotherhood-type tales. Even Nick chimed in. These men had a bond. That much was obvious and they cared about Damon.

"So Damon, we were thinking." Asher leaned forward in his seat. "You've got time to kill while you're off. Let's take a couple of days and go down to my place in the Bahamas. Evie, you, too."

She blinked in surprise. She wouldn't have expected to be included. "You have a house in the Bahamas?"

"On Windermere Island. It's connected to Eleuthera and it's private and secluded. You can really get away and relax there."

She did her best not to moan at the thought of some time on a beach. No John. No threats. Nothing but water and peace.

But these weren't her friends and she didn't belong. In fact, she needed to remember her place. She was on the clock with Damon. She belonged *here*, working on his situation. Not galivanting on a private island with billionaires.

"You should go," she told Damon. "Get away from the stress for a while."

He narrowed his gaze. "And who's going to watch out for you?"

"I am. And if you're that concerned about the safety angle of my place, I can stay here. But you should get away with the guys."

He shook his head. "I need to work out and be ready for when I can return."

Asher turned to Damon. "I have a private gym and a trainer on call. You can work out there and not worry about slacking off. Get checked again by your team doctor when you get back. And Evie, you're coming, too."

Damon leaned back in his seat, his gaze steady on Evie's. "I'll go if you come with me."

She closed her eyes and groaned. How was she going to keep her distance if he insisted on pulling her deeper and deeper into his life? First his mother, now his cousins?

When she didn't answer fast enough, he jumped up, put his beer on the gorgeous rock-like table, strode over, and grabbed her hand.

"Come on. Let's talk." He pulled her to her feet.

She shook her head. "They're your cousins," she said quietly. "And they missed you. Go and—Ack!" she screamed as he knelt down and hefted her over his shoulder.

"We're going to talk," he insisted, striding out of the room to the sound of laughter from the guys.

*   *   *

Damon wasn't one to look a gift horse in the mouth. Asher wanted a trip to his vacation home? Damon had every intention of using the time to get closer to Evie. Yeah, he was still playing the *we're pretending to be a couple* game, and he would until her asshole ex had been caught and locked up. He wanted her mind free and clear to focus on them. But that didn't mean he'd lose this opportunity to be with her.

Not wanting to bicker like an old married couple in front of the guys, he did the only thing he could think of to stop her arguing that he should go by himself. Picked her up and carried her out of the room.

Reaching the kitchen, he slid her down his body and lowered her to her feet. Before she could steady herself, he braced his hands on her waist.

"What the hell was that for?" she asked, outraged.

He shrugged. "I got tired of listening to you insist I go alone. Tell me what I'm going to do by myself on an island when we could get away from the stresses here together?"

She pursed her lips, and it was all he could do not to lean forward and kiss that sweet pucker.

"Damon, I think you're forgetting some important facts."

"Tell me so I can dispute them." He grinned but she didn't smile back, ignoring his attempt to charm her.

"One, you hired me to do a job. And I need to be in Miami to accomplish it. Two," she said before he could open his mouth to dispute her words, "I had a few phone messages that are about upcoming jobs." She folded her arms across her chest, her expression smug and cute, sure she'd made her point. "And three …" She trailed off.

"Out of arguments, huh? Okay, look. I heard you and I respect all your points. But I have a reply for all of your objections. One"—he held up a finger—"I hired you and I can create the parameters of the job. I know you need to find the connection between Emerson's parents and Doc, and you can do that from your laptop in the Bahamas."

She frowned at him but remained silent.

"Two, return the job calls and set up appointments three days from now. And since there is no three, we're going to the Bahamas."

She narrowed her gaze, and he could almost see the steam building inside there. He needed to cut off her anger at his highhandedness. "Don't you want a few days on the beach? Away from our problems?"

She paused at his question. "Well, if you put it that way… But—"

He leaned in and covered her lips with his, kissing her long, deep, and extremely thoroughly. Enough to give her a taste of what their island getaway could be like before raising his head. "So, we're good?"

She cupped his face in her hands. "Do you always get your way?"

He shrugged. "Most of the time. But in this case, it's only because you really want the same thing. You just think you need to argue."

She rolled her eyes. "You're crazy."

"About you." Yeah, he said it, but before she could question him, he yelled to the next room. "We're in! Book the plane."

"Book the plane? What does that even mean?" Evie asked, grasping on to the counter as if she needed to hold on.

"Harrison travels on his private jet. Do we need to go back to your place for bathing suits?" he asked.

She stared at him with those big brown eyes. "What world have I landed in?" she muttered more to herself than to him. "Yes, I need bathing suits."

Shaking her head, she pushed herself off the counter and headed back into the other room.

He knew he'd been fast and her head must be spinning, but he also understood that was the only way he'd get her to go along. Was he still pissed about his career? Yes. Did he still want answers? Of course. But nothing was going to change in a couple of days.

And he could use that time to cement his relationship with Evie.

Chapter Eight

Evie stretched out, relaxed and utterly content. She couldn't remember being anywhere and hearing nothing but crashing waves and blissful silence broken only by occasional masculine laughter or rumbling voices. The beauty of this island defied description. From the blue waters and white sand to the glorious pale-colored mansions, she'd entered heaven on earth.

Although she'd had to be coerced into going, she was happy to be here now, along with the man lying beside her on a double recliner that was as luxurious as any inside bed.

She'd let her family know she was going away for a few days and not to worry if they didn't hear from her. And when she arrived, Damon had encouraged her to shut down her phone and disconnect completely except for the times she chose to work on her laptop.

The guys had sat around most of the day, alternately drinking beer, not their vodka, and lazily tossing a football, Damon watching out for his injury.

She'd dozed off and on to the sound of their

laughter and stories, and she was glad Damon had such solid friendships in his life outside of football. Evie had Quinn, a few acquaintance friends she could go out with on a girls' night, and her four overprotective brothers. All in all, she'd take it and admit to having a good life as well. If not for the return of the jackass she'd been engaged to, that is.

She must have fallen into a deep sleep, because she woke up to the feel of Damon's lips on hers, a low groan reverberating through his big body.

"I thought they'd never leave," he said into her mouth before sliding his tongue between her lips.

"Where'd they go?" she managed to ask.

"Into town for happy hour," he said, delving back in.

"Mmm. Malty. Like beer." And she was a beer drinker. No frou-frou wine for her, and she tangled her tongue with his, tasting her favorite taste.

"I've been watching you in that barely there bikini all day. Hoping the guys were blind. Wanting to throw them into the ocean so I could be alone with you."

She tangled her hands in his hair and pulled on the silken strands. "Then kiss me again."

"Where? Here?" He licked her lips and thrust his tongue inside once more, greedily taking her mouth. "Or here?" He dipped lower, nipping at her collarbone. "Or would you prefer I kiss you here?" He slid the cup of her bikini over her breast, revealing her skin to the warm island air and his waiting mouth.

A flick of his tongue and the pull of his lips that she felt straight down to her clit had her writhing on the cushion.

"Or is it here that you want me to kiss you?" He eased her bottoms down her thighs and off her legs, leaning over to press a kiss on her neatly trimmed sex.

"Yesss," she moaned, arching her hips in a clear entreaty for more. "There."

"No problem." Then he went about what he did best, licking, sucking, and eating at her until she was trembling with desire, her body fighting itself because she couldn't climb fast enough and she needed to peak and fall over that glorious edge.

He gripped her thighs in his big hands and held her legs apart, enabling him to delve inside her with his tongue. Unable to hold back, she cried out at the amazing feel of him, raising and lowering her hips, needing to feel him everywhere. Without warning, he moved, his mouth shifting to her clit, flicking at the tiny nub, and soon she was coming, seeing fireworks behind her closed eyes.

"Damon, God. Yes. Yes." She continued to murmur words, his name, and pleas for more.

He kept going until she peaked and returned to earth. He stood, and before she knew what was happening, he came back over her, notched himself at her entrance, and thrust inside.

She grabbed for his shoulders the minute he entered her because he hit just the right spot and she climaxed once more.

Knowing she was there, he didn't take it slow. He lunged into her, over and over, his deep groans echoing in her ear, the sound of his pleasure arousing on a whole different level.

"Fuck, Evie. You're so tight. So hot. So perfect." Then he shouted as his release took hold and he came hard, the large lounger creaking beneath them.

When he finally rolled off her, she was an emotional wreck from the unexpected emotions soaring through her. She glanced over to find him tying off the condom, and she said a prayer of thanks he'd been coherent enough to think of protection, because she sure as hell hadn't been.

"Evie?"

She met his gaze, shifting her bikini top back in place and sliding on her bottoms. "Yes?"

A sexy smile curved his lips. "Stop overthinking." He rose to his feet in all his naked glory, and she did her best not to sigh as she looked at his tanned, muscular body.

She blinked into the sun, unsure of how to reply. He obviously knew her well or her feelings showed on her face.

"Just enjoy being in paradise, okay?" He picked up a beach bag, obviously ready to leave.

She nodded and began to help him gather their things and head up to the house.

"We'll just go up to our room, shower, and then let me take you for the best lobster dinner you've ever had. Think you can do that?"

"Of course." She shook her head, knowing he was right. For now she was going to have fun. The time to think would come soon enough.

*　　*　　*

Damon sat across from Evie at a restaurant on the ocean. From their seats outside, they could see the rise and fall of the waves as they swept in and out, the scent of saltwater around them. She had a two-pound lobster in front of her, and he had a three-pounder he'd finished in front of him. Although the kitchen staff had cracked the claws before serving, they'd both had to work hard to pull out the meat. With her bib around her neck and a determined expression on her face, she looked adorable.

"So, can I ask you something?" She pulled a leg off the body and sucked out the meat.

Watching her purse her lips was hell on the raging desire that had been plaguing him since they'd arrived on the island. Even their time on the beach hadn't sated his need. But taking her out for a nice dinner had always been on his agenda, and tonight was special.

"Go ahead," he said in a gruff voice.

She met his gaze. "You really didn't care when you found out about your uncle Paul being your biological father?"

He didn't even have to think about it. "Nope." And since she'd brought up the subject of Jesse Prescott, Damon was glad he'd already finished his dinner.

He leaned forward. "Imagine if you did your best but were punished for it because it didn't meet your father's standards. Or you were belittled because the physical part of the game didn't come naturally to you. Or worse, because you weren't as naturally talented as your older brother."

"I'm really sorry," she murmured. "I shouldn't have brought it up."

"Hey, if I'd tell anyone, it'd be you. The thing was, Jesse, my dad, lost out on a pro career due to an injury that sidelined him. He lived for the past and was determined that his kids would damn well succeed where he didn't." Damon took a sip of water. "But later, after finding out about Uncle Paul, I realized there was more to it. Jesse was just a man who felt inadequate about a lot of things, and he took it out on us kids."

When she didn't say anything, he continued. "Each of us was different. Austin was more the golden child. Sports came naturally to him. Jaxon wanted to play baseball and he was damned good at it. You can imagine how well that went over. And Braden…" Damon shook his head. "He was the brain. The smartest one. Now a doctor. But was Dad proud? Hell no. Because he couldn't meet the old man's standards for being a man by playing football."

"He's with Doctors Without Borders, right?" she asked.

"Yep." And Damon was damn proud of his brother.

"What about Bri?" Evie reached out and took his hand across the table.

"He made her play sports. For her he accepted softball and soccer, but she wasn't his focus. She slipped under the radar more than the boys."

A waiter walked over and they both glanced up. "Finished, folks?" he asked.

"Yes, please," Evie said, and Damon nodded.

When the server had removed their dishes, returned, and taken their dessert orders, he left them alone.

"Why did your mother stay with him?" Evie asked.

He rolled his shoulders. It was a question he'd

asked himself many times. "Sometimes I can't figure out whether she loved him or settled because she couldn't have Uncle Paul." He paused. "They grew up together, best friends, and she was in love with him. But you know why that didn't happen."

She looked entranced by the story. "Unrequited love. Or impossible love. Either way, she couldn't have Paul." She paused in thought. "I guess you'll never know the answer to that one."

"Yeah." He knew that. "As for why she stayed? I'm pretty sure she believed she could be a buffer between Jesse and us, but it never worked out that way."

Evie squeezed his hand and he more than appreciated her understanding.

"You know," she said, obviously speaking carefully, "if your mom married Jesse because she couldn't have the person she really loved, that's sad. But I'm sure she thought she wanted a husband and a family. And I would guess she loved him in her own way."

He nodded. "I know. She was and is a great mother."

"And that's why you're a great guy." Evie's smile lit up the room.

"Thanks."

They finished their apple pie a la mode and decided to walk back to the house, hand in hand, taking the route along the beach. He was in shorts, she was in a knee-length dress, and they edged the water, waves lapping over their feet, shoes dangling from their free hand.

After those games of touch football on the beach, his ankle bothered him, aching like it did during a game, making him wish he'd agreed to the shot Doc had suggested. But he wouldn't trade this moment and didn't mind the pain.

Silence surrounded them except for the sound of the ocean. He didn't feel compelled to speak, not after spilling his guts over dinner. He'd often thought about his father's heavy-handed ways and beaten himself up for not living up to Jesse's standards.

Not anymore. He wasn't going to torture himself over his childhood again. Revealing his torment had him looking at his past like an observer. And it had been Jesse's issues, not his, causing him to act like a bully. Jesse's behavior that was wrong, not Damon's or his siblings'.

He glanced at Evie's profile and smiled. She'd lightened his burden. And even better, he hadn't thought about his suspension all night, at least until now, anyway.

And he owed it all to the woman by his side.

*   *   *

The next two days followed the same pattern. Damon worked out in the morning, they had lazy days on the beach, and before dinner, Evie would take an hour or two to do some digging into the college pasts of Gregory Emerson's father and Dr. Jonas. What she'd found was interesting, and she intended to discuss it with Damon on the flight home. No reason to intrude on their vacation when there was nothing to be done. Yet.

She enjoyed another dinner alone with Damon, and they'd had incredible sex in their massively huge bedroom with a king-size bed. Knowing how hard it had been for him to confide in her about his child-hood, she'd treated him to stories of her growing up with four brothers and discovered she and his sister, Bri, had a lot in common. They'd both tagged along with their big brothers, driving them crazy, making them worry about them as they grew up. His father aside, there was as much love in his big family as she had in hers.

She was nervous about the fact that he was certain his mother would follow up with a lunch date, but he assured her his mom was harmless and insisted they weren't lying to her since, *right now*, they were together. And he promised Evie would enjoy his mom. That's what frightened her. She was becoming overly in-volved in Damon's life. Getting to know his friends and family. It was going to be hard to go their separate ways when his case was over and her ex was finally behind bars, where he belonged.

But she put the thoughts out of her head because she had to dress for their last night, when they were meeting the guys for a final get-together before their plane ride home in the morning.

After a delicious meal, they headed back to the house and sat around on the patio overlooking the ocean. The guys smoked cigars, Damon passing because he was in season, regardless of the suspension.

"Damon, have you given any thought to the business proposition we had for you?" Nick, who was mostly silent, surprised Evie by speaking first.

She swung her gaze his way, then glanced at Damon, knowing her curiosity was all over her face.

"We have a new promotional campaign planned for Dirty Dare Vodka, and we want Damon to be the face of the brand. Up until now, he's mostly been a silent partner. We think his mug will sell alcohol, especially to women." Asher winked at Evie. "Think you can convince him?"

"I don't know. Damon?"

Folding his arms across his chest, he shook his head. "I think it's a fucking ridiculous idea. For one thing, my reputation at the moment is shit."

Asher shook his head, then flicked the ash of his

cigar. "This is a blip in time. It's not going to last forever. We can help you rehabilitate your rep. Everyone loves you, Damon. Rise above it and show you aren't in hiding."

Damon frowned at his words. "I'll think about it."

She narrowed her gaze, knowing that meant he'd already made up his mind against it, but she had news that might change how he felt. "So, when I was digging around online, I discovered that Emerson's father and Doc were fraternity buddies at Duke."

Damon's feet, which had been resting on the table, dropped to the floor. "What?"

She nodded. "It's not proof, mind you, but it's a link. And when we were in Doc's office and I asked if he kept in touch with college friends, he never mentioned knowing Emerson's father. That's odd, don't you think?"

Damon's eyes blazed with hope.

"What's going on?" Asher placed his glass on the table and met Evie's gaze. The other two men listened intently.

She sighed. "I'm trying to figure out who benefits from Damon testing positive, and the only person I can come up with is the backup quarterback."

She went on to explain how she'd tested Damon's pain patch because she'd suspected the trainer of giving him drugs, but that had come up empty.

"Anyway, when we went to the doctor the other day, I noticed he attended the same university as Gregory Emerson's father. A little more digging and I discovered they were two years apart but in the same fraternity." Evie couldn't help sounding proud of herself. She was due for a win.

"So you think … what? Emerson got his father to get Doc to slip him PEDs?" Nick asked.

"Something like that. It's just a starting point," she warned them. "But I'm going to prove that Damon is innocent."

The guys stared at her, approval in their eyes and expressions.

She planned to live up to their expectations.

*   *   *

On the flight home, Damon held her hand as they took off. The luxurious jet had a bedroom in the back and plenty of seating, where nobody felt like they were in a sardine can like a typical airplane. Black-and-white marble accented the inside of the jet, and she was in awe of her lavish surroundings.

And with Damon by her side, she was as relaxed as she'd been on the island.

"Back to reality," he said, turning his head to meet her gaze.

She smiled. "Yeah. This was incredible. Thanks for

letting me tag along."

His grin warmed her inside and out.

Evie waited until they landed in Miami to turn on her phone and the messages came pouring in. "What in the world?"

"What's wrong?" Damon asked.

"A lot of messages." Instead of listening to her voicemails, she checked her texts first, her stomach twisting as she read Mack's words. "My apartment was broken into." She clenched her fingers around the phone. "That stupid asshole!"

"What?" Damon stiffened beside her.

She blew out a long breath, trying to analyze and not panic. "I don't have anything of value to speak of, and I'm sure he realizes I haven't been there in days, but you know John wants to scare me."

Damon squeezed her hand. "And did he?"

She shook her head, anger oozing through her veins. "Hell no. I'm sick of him trying to ruin my life."

She rose from her seat and followed everyone down the steps, then turned to the men who'd been so good to her the last couple of days. "Bye, guys. Thank you for including me."

Each pulled her into a warm hug.

Asher's lasted the longest. "If this asshole screws things up, call me." He winked at her and laughed at Damon.

She grinned just as Damon shoved his friend, pushing him away from her.

"We'll stay in touch. Good luck," he said to Damon, then turned to Evie. "Take care of him."

A mixture of emotions floated through her as she wondered for how long she'd have the ability to do just that. "I will."

Then she and Damon headed to the private garage and settled into his car. He pulled out and headed home, still relaxed, driving with one hand on the wheel.

She used the time to call her brother. "Mack?"

"Jesus, Evie. You said you were going to the Bahamas, not off the grid."

"Can't a girl take some time to herself?" she asked. "Before we talk about my apartment, did you find out if the bar had cameras in the back hall?"

"Yes, and you made an excellent call, Evie. We have John on tape with a knife in his hand. We're looking for him. Just stay at Damon's and it'll all be over soon."

She frowned, wishing she knew where to find John herself. But she had no good ideas. She didn't know him now, if she ever really had, and he'd obviously spiraled. But she wanted him caught and her life back. No matter what that meant for her and Damon, she needed to feel composed and in control.

"I'll come to my apartment tomorrow to clean up," she told her brother.

"It's done. Deke, Lucas, Josh, and I pitched in. You're going to have to replace the things John destroyed, but forget about it until he's caught. If you come home, you're an open target, and I'm sure he expects you to show up there. We have a patrol car doing drive-bys, looking out for him. Just sit tight."

"Thanks, Mack. You guys are the best." Her heart warmed for her brothers and how fortunate she was to have them in her life. "You didn't tell Mom and Dad, did you?" She didn't want them worrying.

"Of course not. And don't thank me. In fact, when you hear what I have to say next, you're going to want to kill me," Mack muttered.

Her shoulders stiffened. "What is it?"

He chuckled as he said, "Mom wants us to come to dinner tomorrow night. And she wants you to bring Damon."

"What?" she shouted, startling Damon as he drove. "Sorry, everything's fine," she told him before refocusing on her brother. "Mack, no."

"I'm afraid so. Derek told her you're seeing a famous football player and that John was lurking, but you were safe because you'd moved in with Damon. Of course, she told Dad and they want to meet him." Her brother sounded too amused for her liking.

Her head began to pound. Their pretend game was getting too confused with reality, and her family definitely had the wrong idea about what was going on between her and Damon. "Damon's too busy to be bothered with a family dinner."

"No, I'm not. I'm free whenever," Damon said beside her.

Her gaze slid to his face. A slow grin edged his mouth, and her body reacted because even the man's damned profile was sexy.

She drew a calming breath until her brother spoke again. "I heard that. I'll let Mom and Dad know you'll both be there. Meanwhile, watch your back and I'll see you soon."

Leaning her head back against the plush headrest, she groaned. "You do not want to come to a big family dinner with my parents and brothers," she told him.

He reached over and clasped her hand in his. "Why not?"

"It sends the wrong signal, for one thing."

"You do realize I could hear Mack's loud voice. Your parents already know you're staying with me and we are sleeping together, so we're not really lying."

She shook her head. "You don't understand. They'll think you're serious about me when we know the truth. I know the truth."

"Do you always overthink things? It's a simple dinner with your parents. They'll love me," he said with a charming chuckle.

About that she had no doubt.

＊   ＊   ＊

Damon finished lightweight lifting and exercise at the gym where Jimmy O'Roarke worked out when not with the team. He wished he could press weights harder and be ready sooner even if he couldn't play. Now that he was back home, his anger had returned and he growled his frustration.

"Time will pass," Jimmy said, clearly reading his mood.

He tossed Damon a towel and he wiped his forehead, but there wasn't much sweat to be found. Light workout meant taking it easy. His head felt fine and he had no residual effects from the concussion. That was good news at least.

This morning, when he'd told Evie where he was headed, she informed him she had errands of her own to run. It had taken everything in him not to forbid her from going out alone, but he didn't have the right to issue orders. Worse, if he expressed his objections, she would think he didn't trust her to take care of herself. Instead, he'd reminded her to take her gun, watch her back, and check in before ending his mini rant with a long, distracting kiss that, had they not been in a rush to go, would have ended up in bed.

"Hey. Where'd your mind go?" Jimmy asked.

Damon groaned and forced himself to think of more immediate concerns. "What's your take on Emerson?" he asked his trainer.

Picking up a tumbler with water inside, Damon took a large sip. He didn't want to put any negative thoughts in Jimmy's head. All he wanted was the man's take on the backup quarterback. Jimmy had been a trainer in the league for over ten years and had been around all sorts of players and personalities. Damon wanted his opinion on the man soon to take the field in his place.

Jimmy leaned on a piece of equipment and met Damon's gaze. "I know you're pissed you tested positive and can't start the season. I'm not sure how Greg will perform under pressure, but I know he's going to try his best to make you proud. The kid looks up to you, you know."

"You noticed."

Jimmy chuckled. "Everyone sees it. But I think as shitty as the situation is for you, it's good for him. He'll see what he's capable of." Jimmy put a hand on Damon's shoulder. "And you'll be back leading the offense before you know it."

"Thanks." He paused then decided fuck it. He

wanted to know. "Did Emerson ever mention to you that his father knew Doc back in college?"

Jimmy blinked. "No. That's an odd connection. Huh."

He didn't wonder why Damon had asked and he didn't want to talk smack about Emerson when all he had thus far was coincidence. Two men who'd gone to college together. Frat brothers. But Damon wished he had answers.

His cell rang and he glanced down and grinned. "Gotta take this, Jimmy. I'll see you tomorrow." He hit the accept button. "Braden!" He yelled his brother's name. Braden, Bri's twin, had been out of touch for too long. "Hang on. Let me go somewhere private."

Tucking the phone between his shoulder and cheek, he scooped up his things and headed out for the privacy inside his car. He didn't need a rabid reporter overhearing anything if he spoke in the parking lot.

"Hang on," he said, climbing into the car. He turned on the ignition so the AC would ease the sweating just from walking from the gym to the vehicle. Damn Florida heat. He waited until the phone connected to the car microphone. "Hey, bro."

"Hey! Sorry I've been out of touch. You know I'm in Venezuela, and we're now helping people in Sao

Paulo who don't have access to vaccines."

"Just be careful," Damon warned.

"Always," Braden said. "Anyway, I spoke to Bri this morning," he said of his twin. "I'm sorry for what you're going through and that I haven't been there for you."

Damon rested one hand on the steering wheel. "It's okay. You're out saving the world. I understand."

"But I missed your concussion. Austin's engagement. And I haven't met the baby." He sounded truly upset.

"Are you homesick? Thinking of coming back? You already met your commitment time, so no one would have a problem with you leaving." Damon hoped Braden was finished running.

Though Damon understood why Braden had wanted to get away and live life on terms that had nothing to do with sports, their father had been gone for a long time now, and Braden had nothing more to prove to anyone. Not that he ever had.

"Yes. No. I don't know, okay? I have ties here," Braden said.

Now that was new. "What kind of ties? Colleagues? Patients?"

"Girlfriend."

Damon let out a low whistle. "Is it serious?"

"It's … something," Braden said, obviously vague

on purpose.

"Okay, fine. You don't want to discuss it yet."

Braden laughed. "Do you want to talk about the fact that you have a woman living with you?"

"Fucking Bri," Damon muttered. "She's such a gossip."

"Actually, the information came from Mom first."

He shook his head. "Yeah I've got a woman staying with me. She has some safety issues and I want her where I can keep an eye on her."

"So, you're doing her a favor and the favor actually gets her where you want her," Braden said, guessing the exact nature of the situation.

"You'd like her, man. She's smart and savvy. Not to mention sexy," Damon said.

"And you've got it bad." The connection suddenly sounded gritty.

Damon dipped his head and admitted the truth. "Yeah. I really do."

"Does she?" he asked over light crackling on the line.

Shit. Damon hoped they didn't get disconnected. "She has trust issues I'm working on fixing. An ex who has her afraid to trust, and my past with women isn't stellar. But I'm working on showing her over time." By just being there day after day and proving to her he had staying power.

"Good for you. I have faith you'll get the girl," his brother said.

"And you?"

"Just not ready to share yet," Braden said, making Damon wonder if it was serious or not.

Braden always kept things close. Maybe Bri knew more. They were twins and had a special bond. "Well, I'm really glad you called. And I, for one, hope you come home soon."

Because he really missed his levelheaded sibling.

Chapter Nine

Evie dressed up and drove to the new Miami Thunder Stadium that had recently been constructed, anticipation building inside her. She'd obtained some very interesting information on the team doctor from her computer guru and had put two and two together, knowing the conclusion was good for Damon.

But she hadn't filled him in. She hadn't wanted to get his hopes up in case it was a dead end. Instead she'd called Austin, who'd gotten in touch with Ian. And when the team owner had heard her information, he'd agreed to a joint discussion with Gregory Emerson, the backup quarterback.

She gave her name at security, and a man directed her where to park. She made her way through the parking lot, the summer heat baking down on her, and she could admit to herself she was relieved to be rid of the jacket. Revealing her insecurity in the form of the scar to Damon had given her the courage to walk around without covering it anymore. Did the red line still remind her of her mistakes? Yes. But she needed to learn to live with her past. And maybe she was getting closer to acceptance.

She found her way to Ian's office and she walked up to his assistant's desk. "I have an appointment? Evie Wolfe."

The attractive woman with brown bobbed hair smiled at her. "Of course. One moment, Ms. Wolfe."

Evie waited while the other woman rose from her seat and knocked on Ian's door. "Mr. Dare? Ms. Wolfe is here to see you."

She returned to her chair just as Ian stepped out of his office, formidable in his well-cut suit, a black pin-striped jacket, white dress shirt, and a red tie.

As good-looking as he was, and though he shared the Dare gene for those blue eyes, Evie preferred her men more rugged than polished. Still, there was no denying his dominating presence and sex appeal.

"Evie, good to see you." Ian stepped forward and she extended her hand.

A grin pulled at his lips as he shook it. "How is Damon?" He gestured her to proceed him into his office.

"He's dealing." Her gaze immediately went to the photos on his desk, turned, enabling her to catch a glimpse of his beautiful wife and three young children, two adorable girls and a little boy. "Gorgeous family," she said.

"Thank you. I'm a lucky man."

She settled into a chair across from his desk and eased her legs to one side. She wasn't used to the office-dress look she'd chosen, but she understood her audience. She wouldn't show up here looking like a grungy PI.

"Austin told me about your theory that Gregory Emerson used his connections between his father and our team doctor to drug Damon so Emerson would have the opportunity to prove himself." Ian's stern face was enough to intimidate anyone, but she held her own.

She'd also discovered motive and the connection to make her hunch possible. "Yes, and this morning I found out that Dr. Jonas had IRS issues. He couldn't pay taxes and owed a lot of money. About a month ago, he wrote them a huge check. Some digging into Emerson's father showed he had the same amount going out of his bank account on that same day. Can't be coincidence."

"Son of a bitch. So Emerson's father paid off Doc's debts in exchange for Doc dosing Damon?"

Evie sighed. "That's my theory. Because Damon didn't take drugs. Someone doped him somehow."

Ian studied her intently. "I believe that, too, or I wouldn't even entertain this notion. You've got good connections, Ms. Wolfe."

She grinned. "I manage."

"Look, I don't want to believe Emerson would stoop that low. The kid is diligent, focused, and he works hard. I'd like to speak to him. Handle it my way. I just don't want him to feel like he's being cornered. I've dealt with my share of sports families, and I have my own ideas on how this went down."

She nodded. "However you want to handle it is fine." She was just grateful Ian was being proactive on Damon's behalf.

A knock sounded on the door. "Mr. Dare? Gregory Emerson is here," his assistant said.

"Send him in, Dana."

As Emerson entered, he smiled for his boss, then the grin slid off his face as he realized they weren't alone. "Evie. What are you doing here?" he asked, obviously confused.

"Come sit," Ian said.

"I don't understand." Emerson looked from Evie to Ian and back again.

"Greg, Evie's a private investigator. She's working for Damon to help prove he didn't knowingly take PEDs."

Through narrowed eyes, Emerson asked, "And what does this have to do with me?"

Ian clasped his hands together and leaned forward at his desk. "Did you know your father and Dr. Jonas were frat brothers at Duke?"

"Yes." Emerson let out a slow breath, shoulders slumping. "But I never wanted to get anywhere in my career by nepotism or favoritism, so I don't discuss it. Never told anyone. Ever. As far as I'm concerned, it has nothing to do with me." He ran a hand over his face. "Why is this coming up now? Are you accusing me of something?" He clenched his fists at his sides.

"Not accusing. Asking you flat out. Are you working with Doc to drug Damon so you have a shot to prove yourself?"

"Fuck no!" Emerson slammed his hand on the arms of the chair and propelled himself out of his seat. "And if you think that, fuck you. I won't be disrespected like that." He started for the door.

"Sit," Ian said in his commanding voice. "I believe you." He glanced at Evie. "I've always relied on my gut and this is no different."

Her stomach twisted, feeling like it was plummeting to the floor. "But Damon—"

Ian held up a hand and waited.

Finally, Emerson turned around and met his boss's gaze. "I don't think Damon took PEDs, either."

"Then what do you think happened?" Ian held the other man's stare and, along with Evie, waited for him to reply.

The clock seemed to tick as they sat in silence.

"My father has high expectations," Emerson finally said, shoulders slumped.

Ian rose and walked around his desk, sitting on the corner near Emerson. "And how far would he go for you to meet those expectations?" he asked, his voice deep and low, as if they were the only two in the room.

Emerson swallowed hard. "I guess I need to find out." He looked up at Ian then and glanced over, including Evie. "If my father did anything, not only didn't I know, I don't approve. And I'd gladly step down and give the captain back his starting position on game day."

Suddenly Evie could see why Ian had provided the man the benefit of the doubt. He might be the puppy dog who looked up to Damon, but he was also a man with pride, and he'd grow into himself as an athlete on the team. On his own merits.

"Evie, let me speak to Greg alone. We'll get this sorted out and tell Damon I'll be in touch."

Evie nodded, her mood somber despite being *so* close to clearing Damon she could taste victory.

On her way home, Ian called to let her know Emerson was going to confront his father and get them all some answers.

* * *

Damon had just stepped out of the shower, towel wrapped around his waist, when Evie arrived home. One look at her in a slim black skirt that ended at the knee, a white camisole top, and those red heels he loved so much and his cock perked up, telling him his shower had been a waste of water and time.

"Hey, gorgeous."

She grinned, sitting down on the bed and kicking off her shoes. "Why do women like these things?" she asked with a groan.

"Because they show off those long legs and make me think dirty thoughts." He strode toward her, ignoring the towel when it unhooked from his waist and fell to the floor.

Her gaze locked on his erection that grew more solid the longer she stared. And when she licked her lips, he let out a low growl.

Stepping between her legs, he urged her to lie back on the bed.

"Don't you want to know where I've been?" she asked, breathless, but from the gleam in her eyes, she obviously had something to tell him.

He rose and pulled her up. "Talk while you strip."

She rolled her eyes and pulled off her top. "This morning my computer guy came up with huge news."

He listened as she explained about her meeting with Ian and Emerson and Doc's debts and the check written to him that same day he paid off the IRS. "Jesus. I can't believe he sold me out for cash. Drugged me. Fucked with my career."

"If it's any consolation, Ian and I don't believe Greg knew about it. He was pissed and he's going to confront his father."

Damon lowered himself onto the bed next to her, sex forgotten for the moment. "I know what it's like to have a father who pushes and pushes. If Emerson didn't break under the pressure, he's strong."

Evie placed a hand on his shoulder. "Just like you."

He dipped his head. "I hate to say it, but I can imagine Jesse behaving the same way just to see his sons succeed." He actually felt sorry for the kid.

"Once Emerson hears it from his father, he's going to need understanding. Sounds like you've got plenty of that to offer."

"As team captain, it's part of my job." He glanced at Evie. "I just want the truth to come out. I know it's going to suck for Emerson, but I need my career back and my reputation restored."

She cupped his cheek in her palm. "I think you'll have that soon."

"Thanks to you." This woman had inserted herself into his life and turned it and him upside down in all the best ways.

He hadn't thought they had anything in common, only to find they completed each other in every way.

She stood, shimmied out of her skirt and undies, leaving her only in a bra, which she quickly unhooked. His gaze settled on her heavy breasts and his mouth watered. With one hand on his chest, she pushed him down on the bed, and he maneuvered back to give them more room.

She straddled his hips, knees on either side of him. "You need a condom," she said, rocking her hips and rubbing her sex over his aching dick.

With a groan, he said, "Drawer on my side of the bed." Because the other side belonged to her. Whether she acknowledged that truth or not.

She left him briefly to grab a condom, then returned, ripped it open and rolling it over him. He watched her work diligently, making sure she covered his cock until finally he jerked his hips up.

"Enough. Ride me or I'm going to lose my mind," he said through clenched teeth.

"My pleasure." She lifted her hips and held on to his cock, lowering herself onto his straining shaft.

She slid down and cushioned him in warm, wet heat, causing him to groan. She was heaven and he never wanted to separate from her again.

She began to glide up and down, squeezing her inner muscles tight around him, and the way his body reacted, he wouldn't last long. Thank God she let out a long moan, letting him know she was close, too.

He braced his hands on her hips and began to lift her up and slam her down, grinding them together until his balls drew up tight and he came hard and fast, lost completely. His climax triggered hers, and she spasmed around him, prolonging his ride.

*   *   *

The Wolfe family dinner went as well as could be expected considering Evie sat beside him strung tight. As he sat at the table, her four brothers eyed Damon with a mixture of suspicion and curiosity. He assumed their wariness was a heightened normal after what had happened with John, and he didn't blame them. It showed him where Evie got her distrust from, but still, he had to admit he and his brothers would treat any guy that Bri brought home the same way, especially if the meeting was after she'd been hurt.

Evie's mother, Sunny, had greeted him with a wel-coming hug, and her father, Gary, Damon quickly learned was the silent type unless he had something to say.

"So, Damon, how'd you and Evie meet?" Lucas, the EMT, asked in between bites of the most delicious meatloaf and mashed potatoes Damon had ever eaten.

He could handle this softball question. "Evie's best

friend, Quinn, is engaged to my brother, Austin."

Across the table, her mom looked surprised. "Oh, Evie, I didn't realize Damon was connected to Quinn. You've been quiet about your private life. Ever since John—"

"Mom, we don't discuss the prick," Mack said.

"Language!" she chided him.

Evie's father grunted. "Give me a minute with the son of a bitch."

Ditto, Damon thought to himself.

She stiffened beside him. "Let's not discuss John. I don't want to lose my appetite."

Beneath the table, Damon grasped her hand and squeezed tight.

Josh shrugged. "Okay, subject change. Damon, how do you think Emerson is going to play for the first four games of the season?"

Evie groaned.

Josh shot her an innocent look. "What? Is there a subject that *is* good?"

Deke grinned.

"It's fine. I don't mind talking about it." Damon had expected these kinds of questions. "I think the kid's got a decent arm and he's going to try his best. I'm hopeful."

"Good. We're a Thunder family," Gary said. "So we're obviously happy to have you at our table."

"I appreciate that." He turned to Lucas and Deke. "What's it like to do rescue?" he asked the EMT and firefighter.

With his question, Damon distracted them, and for the next half hour, they talked about various calls they'd gone out on, saves they'd made, and even Mack and Evie's dad shared a few of their more interesting adventures.

After they finished eating, like his mother, Evie's mom had trained her boys to help at the table, so over her protest, Damon helped clean up and bring everything to the kitchen. Before he knew it, they were sitting back down with coffee and dessert.

"If you don't get a lead on John soon, I decided I'm going to move back home," Evie said.

Damon hadn't seen that coming. Neither had anyone else, because every man at the table put his fork down, including Damon. Suddenly her brothers began yelling at once. Knowing it would only hurt his cause, Damon remained silent, which didn't mean he supported her idea. He wanted her where he could keep her safe.

Evie braced her hands on the table, rose to her feet, and yelled, "Quiet!"

Her brothers muttered complaints but did as she said.

"I can't stay with Damon forever. He's been great,

but if things go as we hope, he's going to be back to practice soon. I'll be alone, anyway."

He heard the excuse for what it was. She was definitely using all her self-protection skills to make sure she didn't put her heart on the line. Well, tough shit, he thought. He was in this with her and he'd damn well have a say. Just not in front of her family. She deserved respect for her feelings and opinions on how to live her own life.

"Honey, I know you want to prove you can handle yourself, but John's mentally ill. He's a sick man and we don't know what he'll do next. I felt better knowing you weren't alone," her mother said.

Damon rose to his feet. "I think," he said, hating every word that was about to come out of his mouth, "that Evie knows what's best for her. What if she agrees to install an alarm at the apartment? Will that calm everyone down?"

The brothers and her father grumbled their agreement. "That would be a start," Mack muttered. "I could sleep on your couch and—"

The look Evie shot her brother was deadly.

"Fine." He held up his hands in surrender. "Would you agree to wait a few days? Give me more time to dig and try and find the rock John's hiding under?"

Evie glanced around at her family and nodded, accepting the compromise. "Fine."

"I can't believe you're okay with this," Mack said to Damon.

He wrapped an arm around Evie's waist and pulled her to him. "I trust her judgment and her ability to take care of herself." Which he did.

He just didn't trust her bastard ex.

And what her family didn't know was that Damon didn't intend to let things get as far as her moving out. Not if he could help it.

But for now, she nodded at Damon, surprise and gratitude in her wide, beautiful eyes, and he knew he'd scored necessary points.

"Thank you," she mouthed with obvious feeling.

He smiled back at her. By giving her the freedom she both needed and deserved, he planned to win the war for her heart.

*　*　*

The cool air conditioning blew on her face as Evie sat in Damon's car on the way home. She leaned back against the seat and went over tonight's meal, shocked by how well he'd done with her siblings and parents and twisted up by the fact that he hadn't insisted she stay with him until John was caught.

On the one hand, she was grateful for his support and, on the other, a little disappointed he hadn't insisted she stay. And didn't that say something about her confused state of mind when it came to men in general and a relationship with Damon in particular.

"You held your own with my family," Evie said, breaking the silence. "And thanks for not jumping down their throats when they asked about Emerson."

Damon let out a low, sexy chuckle. "Hey, I expected the questions. I'd have asked them myself if the situation was reversed. Besides, I like your family. They look out for you and that's what's important." He drove with one hand on the steering wheel, every so often glancing her way. "So, you dropped a bomb on everyone tonight."

She curled her fingers into fists beside her. "And you stood up for me. That was also a surprise."

"You didn't think I'd have your back?" He shot her a look before glancing back to the road.

She shrugged, opting for honesty. "I thought you'd hit the roof. Be as worried and upset as they are."

"Who says I'm not worried? And I'm guessing that's why you decided to spring the news on me with everyone else at dinner. You didn't want an argument if you told me when we were alone."

She couldn't help the small smile that lifted her lips at getting caught. "I don't mean to worry you. Or them. I just can't stay with you forever. And an alarm was a brilliant idea. I was going to ask my landlord for permission, anyway. I don't mind giving Mack a few more days to do his job. I can't think of where John would go, so I'm going to leave it to Mack and focus on getting you back on the field." Make sure Ian had everything he needed to go to the league on Damon's behalf.

Damon cleared his throat. "I'm going to be honest with you. I don't think an alarm is enough of a solution, because I don't trust that bastard John at all." He paused before continuing. "But I do trust you. And you're right. I can't keep you locked away in my house for the rest of your life."

She swallowed hard, not knowing what to say. Because in his house was exactly where she wanted to be. But trusting him not to change his mind later and hurt her wasn't easy.

"I'm exhausted," she said, bed calling her. After the long day she'd had, she needed to crash and deal with all her conflicting emotions in the morning.

* * *

Damon answered his door in the morning to find Ian Dare and Gregory Emerson on the other side. "Well, this is a surprise."

"Sorry to just show up, but I figured you were going to want to hear what we have to say," Ian said. "Mind if we come in?"

Beside him, Emerson appeared subdued and silent.

"Of course." Damon gestured for them to step inside, shut the door behind him, and led them to the family room.

He'd have called for Evie to join them, but she was showering upstairs.

"Coffee? Water? Anything to drink?" he offered the men.

"Nothing for me," Ian said, taking a seat on the sofa.

"Emerson?"

The other man shook his head. "No, thanks. I'd rather get this over with." He lowered himself on the far end of the couch.

Damon narrowed his gaze but he couldn't bring himself to sit. "Okay then. I assume this is about you setting me up?" He clenched and unclenched his fists. This was something he hadn't let himself deal with emotionally, because without proof, he had no way of getting those four games back. And that's what he wanted, along with his reputation.

"When Evie called me and brought to light the connection between Greg's father and Doc, the hairs on the back of my neck stood up. I knew something was off but I never thought Emerson was behind it."

Damon's head began to throb. "So, what happened exactly?"

Emerson lifted his gaze. "My old man happened.

He did some digging and discovered Dr. Jonas owed the IRS a lot of money. He went to see him and Doc admitted to having gambling issues. My dad, who wants me to succeed any way he can, offered to pay Doc's debt to the IRS—"

"If he dosed me so I'd test positive…" Damon shook his head but he actually felt sorry for the guy. Like he told Evie, he knew exactly what it was like to have a domineering asshole father. "How'd he know they'd test me? Those are random."

Ian groaned. "This kid's father has connections like you wouldn't believe."

"So this goes higher up?" Damon asked in disbelief.

"What can I say? It's easy to find dirt on people, and my father has enough money to do it." Emerson rose to his feet, hands in his sweatpants pockets. He looked beaten down. "I've already gone to the commissioner. He's calling the cops. And I'm sure you'll be reinstated soon."

Although Damon knew he ought to be happy at the news and pissed at the situation in the first place, all he could feel was pity for Emerson, who'd had to turn his own father in.

A knock sounded and Damon turned toward the entrance to the family room, where Evie stood. Her gorgeous hair fell over her shoulders and her makeup-free face made him grin. She was dressed like Evie the PI, the real woman who made him burn. He was head over heels, that was for damned sure.

"Sorry. Am I interrupting?" she asked.

Ian, the only one left sitting, rose from his seat. "Come on in, Evie. If it weren't for you, we wouldn't have made the connection." He went on to explain to her how Damon had ended up testing positive for PEDs. "Congratulations. You cracked the case." Ian extended his hand, and she bounced over to accept his shake before turning to Emerson.

"I'm sorry," she said.

"Not your fault. I'm glad Captain was cleared. I understand if you want me out," he said to Ian.

The team owner walked over and put a fatherly arm around Emerson's shoulders. "Since when are we responsible for the mistakes of our parents? If that were the case, I'd be shit out of luck in life."

Ian's father, Robert Dare, had been a son of a bitch and probably would have gotten along well with Jesse Prescott. In Robert's case, he'd had one legitimate family with a woman he'd married, Ian's mom. Without anyone knowing, he'd had a mistress with kids on the side. After a lot of drama, the kids were all close now and estranged from their father.

"Apparently we can all understand asshole parents," Damon muttered. "Emerson, I don't blame you for what your father did." He strode over and put a hand on the dejected man's back.

"Thanks."

"I have an appointment with a potential client. I need to go," Evie said.

"I think my car is blocking yours. And we said what we came to say." Ian nodded toward Emerson. "Ready?"

He nodded. "Sorry again."

Evie met Damon's gaze, her eyes alight with pleasure. Sure, she'd solved how Damon had been drugged, but he sensed there was more.

That she was happy for him.

Chapter Ten

After Ian and Emerson left, Damon called Austin and asked him to come over so he could fill him in. They sat on his back patio by the pool, and he felt as if a weight had been lifted off his shoulders. He'd be back with his team as soon as the suspension was removed, and his dignity and reputation would be restored.

"It sucks, man. I can see Jesse pulling such a dumb-ass stunt to get one of us an opportunity we either weren't ready for, didn't deserve, or hadn't yet earned," Damon said, speaking the thing he couldn't get off his mind. "And Emerson's going to have to live with what his old man did."

Austin rolled his shoulders. "You got through it, but did you put it behind you?"

"I thought I did but this whole situation stirred up a lot of shit. After I tested positive, memories of how Dad would make me feel when I disappointed him ran through my head. Now this situation with Emerson and his father ... I think it'll always be with me one way or another. I've just started to realize that the blame lies on him and not me."

Austin put a hand on his shoulder. "Good. You know I'm always here to listen. So is Uncle Paul. The man's got a good heart, and I know if it weren't for his counterbalance of Dad, life would have been harder."

"Yeah, I know." And Damon did. Some people weren't as lucky. He stretched his legs out in front of him, letting the sun hit his skin.

"I've also got Quinn. She centers me."

Damon felt his brother's pointed stare and groaned. "Just ask, okay?"

With a shrug, Austin nodded. "Okay, what's going on with Evie?"

He stared up at the blue cloudless sky. "I wish to hell I knew. I believe she feels the same way I do about her, but she's got walls a mile high."

"From what Quinn tells me, she's got good reason to be wary, but damn, you're solid."

Frowning, he picked up a sports drink he'd left on the table beside him. "Hasn't seemed to matter. Maybe once this shit with her ex is over, when he's caught, she'll let her guard down." He took a sip from the bottle. "There's also the little fact that I've never had a relationship. Maybe she doesn't believe I can settle down."

Austin chuckled. "Hell, if I did, you can."

"Truer words, brother. Truer words. So, when is

the wedding?" Damon asked.

"We haven't gotten that far. You try planning with a baby."

"Whoa." Damon held up both hands. "Let me get the girl first, would you?"

With a shrug, Austin said, "It worked for me the other way around."

Damon rolled his eyes just as his cell phone rang. He caught Evie's name on the screen and took the call. "Hey, beautiful."

"Damon, I'm at the police station. I had a run-in with John."

Ice ran through him with no regard to the heat from the sun. "Are you okay?"

"I'm fine."

He told himself to relax but it didn't work. "Text me the address. I'll be right there. Then call Mack." He disconnected the call and turned to his brother. "I've got to go. Evie had a run-in with the asshole."

"Want me to tag along?" Austin rose from his seat, but Damon shook his head.

"I've got it, but thanks." He pulled his brother into a brief hug. "Tell Quinn we'll get in touch when I know what's going on," Damon said, knowing Austin's next move would be to call his fiancée and Evie's best friend.

He sped to the address she texted him, shocked he

didn't get ticketed on the way.

*   *   *

Evie pulled out of Damon's driveway behind Ian's luxury vehicle and headed to a Starbucks coffee shop a town away from Miami, about fifteen minutes from Damon's house. A woman's teenage daughter had run away six months ago, and the police were out of leads. She wanted to hire Evie to see if she could track her child down or find clues the police had missed. After an hour with the distraught woman, Evie was determined to help her.

Coming off the high of Damon's case and success, her adrenaline was pumping through her veins. She bought herself a cup of coffee to go. Despite the summer heat, she liked her coffee hot, and she walked back to her car, parked behind the row of stores.

She'd forgotten to take her keys out of her purse and had to juggle her coffee, putting it down on the top of her car so she could dig through her handbag. Which wasn't easy because, since living with Damon, she'd taken to carrying way too much around in her purse.

She was rooting around inside when she heard him.

"I knew I'd get you alone again."

At the sound of John's voice, she dropped her bag

to the ground and reached for her gun, pulling it from her waistband. No sooner had she raised the weapon than he gripped her wrist in his big hand. Knowing better than to fight him since he was stronger, she released her grip, letting the weapon fall. She immediately swiped the coffee cup from the top of her car and flipped off the lid.

He'd sunk down to retrieve the gun, and she moved fast, throwing the steaming hot coffee into his face.

He screamed, his hands coming to his cheeks. "You bitch!"

They'd drawn a crowd but she didn't care.

"I'm a bitch?" she yelled at him. "You've been stalking me for months, invaded my privacy, drove me out of my own apartment, and attacked me with a knife. Twice. And I'm a bitch?" She drew her leg back and nailed him in the balls just as a cop pulled up and a man she didn't know put a hand on her shoulder to distract her before she went after John again.

Despite the fact that she was licensed as a PI and had a permit for the gun, she'd been taken to the police station to give a statement and press charges. Though she hadn't realized there were witnesses before she'd made a scene, a man had seen John approach her first, and nobody was willing to admit to seeing her kick her ex in the balls despite John's whining and claim. The coffee had been self-defense.

Luckily, her brother Mack was nearby on a call and said he'd meet her at the station where she'd been taken. And though she told herself not to rely on Damon, she'd called him first and wasn't surprised when he came running in soon after Mack.

"Evie!" Damon called out her name and she flew out of her seat and into his arms. "Jesus, what happened?" he asked as he ran a hand over her hair, then pulled her in front of him to inspect her and make sure she was really okay.

She couldn't control the grin that lifted her lips. "I kicked John's ass, that's what. I saw him and pulled my gun. He grabbed my wrist and I outsmarted him. I dropped the gun, took him off guard, and tossed my hot coffee in his face."

"He's still in booking crying," Mack muttered. "Claims she nailed him in the balls, too, but there's nobody willing to corroborate his story." He winked at his sister.

Evie grinned wider.

Damon shook his head, a proud expression on his face. "You're pressing charges?"

"Damn straight."

"I'm telling you she attacked me!" John's voice sounded loudly around the room.

She turned to see a uniformed police officer escorting John from the back room. He dove toward her and the cop yanked him into place beside him. "Sorry, folks. Taking him to a holding cell."

Damon walked away from Evie and strode over to her ex. The holding officer's eyes opened wide. "You're Damon Prescott. I'm a huge fan, as is my son. Can I get an autograph for him?" the cop asked.

"You got it. Before you take this prick, can I have a word?"

The officer nodded and discreetly looked away, keeping a hold on John, who was in cuffs.

John's eyes were huge with a touch of fear, and Evie got a lot of satisfaction from his panic.

"You touched my girl," Damon said, stepping into John's personal space. But he didn't speak low. "Listen good. If you ever go near her again, if you look at her again, if you so much as blink her way, you won't see me coming. But you will regret it."

Damon glanced at the officer. "Thanks, man. I'll leave an autograph for your son and a phone number. I'll get you set up with tickets to a game, too."

"Hey, thanks!" The officer grinned. "Let's go," he said in a commanding voice to his prisoner.

"He threatened me!" John yelled.

"I didn't hear a damn thing, buddy. Now move it." He gave John a shove and herded him across the room and through a door leading, she assumed, to holding cells. She didn't care as long as he was out of her life, and she'd do whatever she had to in order to make sure he didn't get another *deal*. Given how he'd lost his status since the last arrest, she was hoping there wouldn't be an issue and he'd go away for a while this time.

Damon and Mack waited while she gave her statement to the officer. Both men refused to leave, and out of respect for Mack's position and Damon being who he was, they let them stay with her while she was questioned.

Unsure how much time had passed, they walked out of the police station and back into the Florida sunshine.

Mack put an arm around her shoulder. "You okay?"

She looked up at her big brother and smiled. "Better than I've been in a long time."

Nodding, he sighed in relief. "Then I'm leaving you in good hands," he said, glancing at Damon. "You've got this?"

"Of course."

"See you guys later." Mack nodded his head and strode off, headed to his car.

Left alone with Damon, she realized that with his case resolved and John finally behind bars, the main reasons for them being together had been wrapped up.

Her need to stay with him was finished. Their short-term, *this is fun* fling? Probably over, too.

Except she recalled what he'd said to John. And she wasn't ready to say goodbye, which was the antithesis of what she should be feeling. What every wall she'd built around her heart told her she should be feeling. But this was Damon, the man who'd been by her side every step of the way in dealing with John. Who'd supported her. Who seemed to show her he cared.

She turned to him, ignoring the people rushing by on the sidewalk, and met his gaze. Drawing on the bravery that had gotten her this far today and the words he'd said when he'd confronted John, she stepped closer and wrapped her arms around his neck.

"Did you call me your girl?"

His hands slid to her waist and he pulled her against him. "You know it. You can fight it all you want, Evie, but you're mine."

She had insecurities and questions that went along with that statement, but for now, she rose to her tiptoes and sealed her mouth over his. He speared his tongue between her lips and kissed her senseless on the sidewalk in front of the police station.

"Hey, take it inside," a female voice said.

Blushing, Evie pulled back to find a woman rushing by with her little boy. "Sorry!" she called after her but the mother ignored her.

Damon looked at her and grinned. "I say we take this to the bedroom."

"Umm, my car's at the coffee shop parking lot," she said. "I was brought here by the police."

He shook his head. "We'll come back for it later."

She nodded, wanting this time with him and knowing they needed to talk.

She slid her hand into his. "Lead the way."

*   *   *

If Damon could freeze this moment in time, he would. Buried inside Evie's warm body, knowing she was safe, that his life was almost back on track thanks to her, well, it was perfection. She was perfection. Now if he could just find a way to keep her here.

A little while later, he lay sated, Evie curled in his arms. He could almost hear the gears turning in her brain. "Just this once I'm going to let you overthink things. What's going on in that head of yours?" he asked, tangling his fingers through her hair.

She sighed. "Okay, well, your case is almost finished. At least my part in it is."

He nodded.

"And my situation is resolved. No need to hide out here for protection."

"Nope. You no longer *have to* be here," he agreed.

"But there's been more to us than just those two things."

"Right. We've been having fun and enjoying the moment," she said.

Which was the crux of the problem. He'd agreed to what amounted to an affair because he knew she'd never admit to wanting more. But now he was ready to push and push hard. He knew how happy she'd been that he'd called her his girl. He just had to get her to see that he was all in.

"Except we turned into something more and you don't want to face it." Calling her out on her fears was the first step.

She froze in his arms.

"Are you going to deny it?" he asked.

She shook her head and pressed her lips against his chest.

"Good, because I know how I feel about you. I love you, Evie Wolfe."

Obviously startled, she sat up in the bed, pulling the sheet up to cover her breasts. "You *love me*?"

"I love you and I want a life with you." He held his breath as she absorbed his words.

The color drained from her face. "I … I didn't see this coming."

"Because you didn't want to see. But we're good together. We click on every level, so why can't we give a serious relationship a shot?" God knows he'd been doing it for almost the entire time they'd been together.

Her fingers curled around the sheet. "I'm scared. You'll be reinstated any day, and your life will go back to full-time football."

She licked her lower lip and he stifled a groan. "So?"

"So, you won't have time for a girlfriend, and let's face it, you've never wanted or tried a relationship before. Now add the pressure of a contract year? It's a recipe for disaster."

She went to slide out of bed, but he stopped her, grasping her wrist. "I get that you're scared. John didn't give you a reason to believe in relationships or men in general. You want to push me away before I hurt you but I'm not going to let you."

"No?"

He heard the hope in her voice. "No. Now listen to me.

I may not have a ton of time during the season, but you'd be my priority when I'm not working. And you don't strike me as a needy type that would resent my job." He raised his eyebrow. "Unless I've read you all wrong?"

She shook her head, happy tears in her eyes. "No. You didn't read me wrong. I'm just such a mess since

John and suddenly it's over. And I can look ahead."

"And what do you see?" he asked gruffly.

"I know what I *want* to see. Us."

He couldn't stop the grin that took hold. "Yeah? And why's that?"

She slid back across the bed and pulled herself on top of him. Her warm skin seeped into his pores. "Because I love you, too."

No sooner had she spoken than she found herself on her back, Damon buried deep inside her once more, and this time, when he moved, she opened her heart and let him in.

*   *   *

I love you, too. Evie couldn't believe she'd said the words out loud. She'd barely admitted them to herself, but they were true, and she'd been pushing aside her feelings for Damon for weeks, coming up with excuses to keep him at a distance. Although she had to admit she was worried about him maintaining a relationship during the season, especially since he'd never attempted one before.

"I have a solution to your concern." Damon lay back, one arm propped behind his head.

Rolling to the side, her own elbow propping her up, she replied, "What's that?"

"Move in with me for good. That way, when I'm

here, you're here. Let's just do this thing, because there's no other way I can prove to you that I'm all in."

Move in? As in give up her apartment? Pack up all her things and—

"This is one of those times I won't let you overthink. You're already here. Just stay. And yes, we can pick up more of your things. As much or as little as you want. And when you're ready, you can sublet your apartment."

Evie told herself not to hyperventilate. This man had already proven himself to her. All she needed to do was trust in herself and take the leap. "Okay."

"Yes!" He pumped his fist and pulled her on top of him and into a kiss. "I love you and I'm going to show you what a great life we can have."

She smiled and kissed him back. "I believe you."

*   *   *

Evie strode into the Miami Thunder Stadium beside Quinn and Austin. The rest of the Prescotts met them in the box, Bri with Macy, Jaxon was now in his post-season and free to attend, and Christine Prescott, along with Paul and Ron.

Also joining them were various Dare couples and some of their kids. Since Evie had been coming to every home game for the last three months, she'd met all sides of the Dare-Prescott family. From Robert Dare's legitimate children and their spouses to his *other* children, Evie was getting to know them all well. Even Ian, who alternated between the owner's box and the family one.

Evie sat up front, waiting for the team to do their run out onto the field. She was early for game nine, a week before a bye – a day off – next weekend.

As they'd hoped, Damon had been cleared to play before game one. Doc and Emerson's father had been arrested on an array of charges along with those responsible for scheduling Damon's "random" drug test.

As for John, though his lawyer had wanted him to plead insanity, John himself had all but given up. He'd agreed to plead guilty and had been sentenced to ten years in prison as it hadn't been his first offense. Without the need to testify at trial, Evie was free of him.

Quinn joined her, pulling up a chair by the glass in front of them.

"Is it me or is it more crowded than usual in here tonight?" Evie asked, looking around at Damon's family crowding the room.

Ian's siblings congregated in various groups, the kids tugged on their parents' arms, begging for food, and Jaxon stood with Bri and Macy, his gaze on the beautiful blonde.

As Evie had learned in the last couple of months, Jaxon was a bad boy and a partier but a solid man and brother. Despite his age, he was an amazing pitcher for the Miami Eagles and a devoted brother. According to Austin, at twenty-eight, with surgery behind him, Jaxon was nearing the end of his career on the field. Something he refused to acknowledge or face.

The man was also an extreme flirt with anyone in a skirt. Or jeans, in the case of Macy Walker, who was laughing at something Jaxon had said, but it was obvious she didn't take him seriously. If she didn't read the tabloids, no doubt she knew his reputation from Bri.

"I guess everyone wants to see the game." Quinn answered Evie's question, grinning when she looked Evie over. "Nice shirt."

"Hey, I have to represent," Evie said, turning to show her friend Damon's number eleven on the back of Evie's jersey and the name Prescott across her shoulders.

Quinn, who had left Jenny at home with her niece/babysitter because of the ungodly noise in the stadium, merely laughed. "That's a far cry from the woman who was running away even when you were living with the man."

"Hey, pot, kettle," Evie said, calling out Quinn for

doing the same thing, trying to keep Austin at an emotional distance even after she'd moved in to help him with Jenny.

"Well, it all worked out for me." Quinn held up her hand and admired her ring, which was freaking gorgeous but too big for Evie's taste. Something more simple would suit her... Wait. What the hell was she thinking?

Life was great now. She'd never left Damon's and had been living with him ever since. Over the last three months, they had moved almost all of her clothing and personal items into his house. They'd even brought over some other favorite pieces of furniture that Damon could fit into the SUV he'd purchased. He'd given up using their small cars after one too many trips in a day.

He'd been correct. Living with Damon meant he could spend his free time with Evie. True, he didn't sleep at home the night before Miami games when the team stayed in a hotel or when they had away games. And his schedule was insane. But she kept plenty busy. Thanks to her work on Damon's case, her name had been mentioned around the NFL, and she had bigger clients now. And Damon worked hard to allay any fears she'd had about him not adjusting to a relationship.

And he liked her just as she was. She glanced down

at her scuffed black boots beneath her jeans. He complained when she overdid makeup, thinking she needed to impress him in any way. He loved her. Period.

Warmth filled her and she couldn't help but smile.

She heard familiar voices and turned to see her brothers and parents making their way toward her. She jumped up from her seat. "What are you all doing here?"

Before they could answer, music sounded, coming from the field, and she spun back in a rush, not wanting to miss the team's charge. To her surprise, all she could see was one man in the center of the field. Suddenly every screen above the stands lit up and she realized it was Damon.

She could see him up close, and then she heard his voice over the microphone. "Indulge me, everyone."

"What's happening?" Evie looked around the room to find all eyes shifting from Damon to her. She glanced back at the screen to see him grinning. "Have you figured it out yet, Evie?"

She narrowed her gaze, her heart pumping in her chest.

"In case you haven't…" He took out a ring box and got down on one knee. "Remember when you were worried I would change my mind about wanting a relationship with you? That football would get in the way of us? I think we've had enough time for you to see nothing will get in our way."

Behind her, her mother squealed.

Beside her, Quinn looked at her with tears in her eyes and happiness on her face. The same expression Evie probably had had when Austin proposed to Quinn.

"These Prescott men have a flare for the dramatic, don't they?" she asked, cheeks burning, her eyes also filling.

"Marry me, Evie Wolfe."

Leave it to Damon not to ask but to state what he wanted.

The crowd erupted in a roar.

"Yes!" She waved from the box, which was caught on the screen.

"Get down here!" he yelled.

She worked her way through the family members, who she now understood had come for the proposal. She'd have time with everyone during the game. The immediate moment was for Damon. She bolted out of the box and rushed down toward the field. All the while, she heard the clapping and whistling of the Thunder Stadium spectators.

Finally, she reached the tunnel, where a security guard was waiting for her and escorted her to the field. And then she ran until Damon swooped her into his arms and spun her around.

Dizzy, happy, and in love, she grinned as he settled her on her feet and held out the open box. "So, you know I wanted to outdo Austin," he whispered in her ear. "But I know you."

She looked down and stared at a sapphire emerald-cut stone with small diamonds on either side. Perfect for her, and the tears she'd been holding back began to fall.

"Oh, Damon!"

He slid the ring on her finger and pumped his fist for the home crowd.

"I couldn't think of a better way to show you I'm in it forever."

She grasped his cheeks and pressed her lips to his. "I love you, Damon. Thank you for understanding me. Getting me. Loving me."

"I love you, Evie."

She grinned. "Now go play ball."

Epilogue

D amon's mother threw an impromptu engagement party for him and Evie at her house, squeezing in a small amount of family and friends, since Damon's team had a bye week and didn't have to play that weekend. The only sibling missing was Braden, who couldn't get away from his obligations.

The celebration was at the home Christine had finally relented and allowed her children to buy for her in light of their individual successes. The five-thousand-square-foot ranch had rooms for her adult kids to stay over if they chose, a pool in the backyard, and a huge open-concept layout inside. For that reason, it was perfect for a family gathering.

Christine, who'd already won over Evie and vice versa, shocked everyone by bringing a date, Edward Madison, a businessman who she'd met at a game last year.

"Mom, Edward, this is a surprise," Damon said, Evie by his side, holding his hand. And when he glanced down, he noticed his mother's and Edward's hands were also entwined.

"Well, we wanted to see what we had in common before we went public," she explained.

"And we discovered we're extremely compatible." Edward, who had dark blond hair and brown eyes, smiled at Damon's mother in a way Damon would want someone to look at her, and the twisting in his stomach eased.

Still, he had to take a mental step back and decide how he felt about his mom in a relationship after all this time and realized all he wanted was for her to be happy. Studying her glow as she looked at Edward, he approved.

"Thanks for the party," Evie said with a bright smile. Ever since her ex had pled guilty, her entire demeanor and mood had been lighter.

"You're welcome. It's completely my pleasure. Welcome to the family. You're going to fit right in. Now you two go mingle." His mom shooed them away to enjoy their party.

Instead of finding friends or family to talk to, Damon snuck Evie into a hallway where they could have a few minutes alone.

Bracing his hands on her hips, he pulled her to him. "Don't get me wrong. I love you in jeans and tight tanks and tee shirts, but every once in a while, seeing you in a dress and fuck-me heels works, too."

She treated him to a sexy grin. "Kind of like the

difference between me seeing you in your tight-ass jeans and your football uniform. Either view works for me." She rose up and kissed him, but he wasn't content with a peck on the lips.

Hooking his arm around her waist, he yanked her against him and turned her light kiss into a soul-deep melding of minds and hearts. He slid his hands into her long hair and tugged her neck into the position he wanted her. Then he tangled his tongue with hers and lost himself in everything he'd never known he wanted but now couldn't live without. He didn't know how long they remained hidden, making out like teenagers, and he didn't care.

"Hey, you two. Either go to a bedroom or come hang with everyone celebrating your engagement," Jaxon called out, deliberately walking over and interrupting them.

Damon took his time extricating himself from Evie and then stepped in front of her, giving her time to pull herself together.

He studied his brother, whose eyes were red-rimmed and his hair long, probably because he was in the off-season. His baseball team demanded a haircut above the collar and no facial hair. Left to his own devices, Jaxon would look a lot more raggedy.

"Hey, man. Are you hungover?" It was a rhetorical question. Damon knew his brother liked to party.

Jaxon rubbed his eyes. "Just a late night," he said, his lips lifting in an *I got some* grin.

Damon shook his head and chuckled. "Okay, who was she?"

Evie stepped out from behind Damon, her hair still messed, but he knew his girl. She wouldn't care.

"Yeah, Jaxon. Who's the lucky lady this time?" Evie teased. Because everyone knew Jaxon wouldn't settle down with just one woman. He'd been burned in the past and hadn't let it go.

"Just a chick I met at Allstars last night," Jaxon said.

Damon understood why Jaxon would choose the upscale bar instead of a place where he'd be surrounded by groupies.

Damon put a hand on the back of his brother's neck and pushed him forward. "Well, let's go get you some caffeine, bro. You look like you could use some." He loved his brother even if they were very different.

Grinning, Evie walked along beside them. They almost bumped into Bri and her friend Macy as they reentered the main room.

"Hi," Macy said, champagne in hand. Her gaze encompassed the three of them.

Bri looked everyone over, his big sister curious as ever.

"Hi, ladies," Jaxon said. "You're looking good, Macy. White enhances your tan. Hot." He'd perked up at the sight of her.

Damon raised his eyebrows at Evie, who merely shrugged. Obviously she didn't know any more about Jaxon and Macy than he did. Then again, his brother could just be acting like his normal flirtatious self, which all the Prescott men did or had done in their single days.

"Thanks, Jaxon." Macy didn't even blush at the compliment.

Damon figured she had his brother and his behavior pegged and didn't take him seriously. Good. He'd hate to see Jaxon hurt his sister's friend. Not that Jaxon would do anything deliberately, but he was a player. A good man but one who liked women. Plural.

"So, what were you three whispering about?" Bri finally asked.

"Just asking Jaxon what he's been doing," Damon said.

"You mean *who* he's been doing," Bri said, a knowing smile on her lips and loud enough for them all to hear. "Come on, Macy. Let me introduce you to a few people from work. I think you'll like Adam Martsoff." She steered her friend away from Damon, Evie, and Jaxon.

"Something I said?" Jaxon asked.

Damon shook his head. "Just protecting her friend from your charms, bro." Though Damon still hoped the right woman would straighten out his brother's ass one day.

In the meantime, Damon would celebrate the fact that *he'd* found the woman of his dreams. The rest of the party passed with Damon and Evie accepting congratulations from their families and, at the end, saying goodbye to each grouping one by one.

Finally, they came to the last couple except for Damon's family and a few friends who had remained behind.

Ian and his wife, Riley, walked over.

"Congratulations!" Riley, a bubbly brunette with curly brown hair pulled first Evie, then Damon into a hug.

"I wish you all the best," Ian said. "And if your life is anything like mine, you'll be one happy man."

Riley laughed. "He's happy because all the kids are home with a babysitter. He's got time to breathe. Then he'll go home and let them hang all over him and love every minute of it."

"I'm happy for you as well," Damon said. From what he understood of his boss and cousin, Ian Dare had become the man of the house when his father revealed he had another family, and as a result, Ian hadn't believed in love. Then he'd met Riley and become a changed man.

Damon understood. Evie had altered him in every way.

From across the room, they heard yelling, and everyone turned to see what was going on. "We're going to get going and let you deal with that," Ian said, gesturing to where Jaxon and Bri were in a heated discussion that had grown loud enough to cause people to look their way.

"Thanks for coming." Damon shook Ian's hand.

Then he and Evie headed toward the commotion. "What's wrong?" he asked.

"Ask Jaxon." Bri folded her arms across her chest and glared at their brother.

Macy, who hadn't left, stood beside Bri and watched in obvious shock and wonder.

Jaxon flushed a healthy shade of red. As Damon glanced around, he saw his mother looking concerned, Edward comforting her, Austin obviously gritting his teeth while Quinn, baby in her arms, tried to talk him down.

Damon turned to Evie. "Let me talk to him." He gestured to Jaxon.

She nodded and headed to Damon's mother, no doubt to help soothe her.

"Come on, let's go have a talk," Damon said to his sibling.

Bri shook her head. "You're not leaving me out of this. I'm his publicist and he's damn well going to need one."

"Why?" Damon asked, feeling protective of Jaxon.

Jaxon opened his mouth to explain, when Bri chimed in first. "You know that *chick he met at Allstars last night*?" she asked, using air quotes.

"Yes?" Damon asked warily.

"It turns out she's his general manager's daughter, home from college for a long weekend."

Damon's eyes opened wide. "Dude!" Even he was surprised at his brother's behavior.

"She's twenty-one and legal!"

"That doesn't make Brett Majors any happier with you," Austin said, coming up beside them. "Someone caught you two on a cell phone video grinding away while making out in the back hall of Allstars. And despite the fact that the owner demands discretion and privacy, the person leaked the video."

Macy gasped, caught herself, blushed, and took a step back. If she held any interest in Jaxon, this ought to douse her attraction, Damon thought.

"And to say the video has gone viral is an understatement." Bri glared at Jaxon, whose behavior had finally caught up with him.

He rubbed the back of his neck, his stress obvious.

Damon, who had just been in the basement with

his own team, albeit through no fault of his own, knew what kind of trouble Jaxon was in and felt for him, putting a hand on his brother's shoulder.

Austin cleared his throat. "We are not doing this here. Not today. Today is Damon and Evie's celebration," he said, glancing at them before turning back to Jaxon. "I can guarantee you that you're going to be called into a meeting with the owner, manager, and GM and it will not go well." He shook his head. "Bri and I will figure out how the hell to fix this mess."

Even Damon winced at the demand and anger in his oldest brother's tone. This was sports agent Austin Prescott, not anyone's big brother. And Jaxon was in serious trouble.

But Austin was right. Today was his and Evie's day and Damon turned to his fiancée who had joied him. "What do you say we duck out and head home?" Where he knew exactly what he wanted to do with the woman he loved.

Her beautiful smile lit him up inside. "After we say goodbye and thank you. No ducking out," she chided him, patting him on the cheek.

As usual and to Damon's frustration, the last goodbyes took a while, but finally he found himself at home, naked with Evie in his bedroom, his body buried deep inside hers. Where he belonged.

Thanks for reading! Continue this series with Dare to Play!

Keep reading for a sneak peek!

DARE TO PLAY EXCERPT

"There is a lot of testosterone in this room." Macy Walker glanced around the living area of Christine Prescott's home and let out a low whistle.

Most of the guests were jocks dressed up for Damon Prescott and Evie Wolfe's engagement party, their asses tight and faces gorgeous. Macy had to admit she'd come up in the world since meeting Brianne Prescott at an exercise class and becoming fast friends.

"Eew." Brianne wrinkled her nose in disgust at Macy's comment. "Three of those men are my brothers you're talking about."

"Oh come on. Besides them. Look around you. You can't deny the hotness."

Brianne, a publicist at Dare Nation, a sports agency owned by her brother and uncle, was used to dealing with professional athletes while Macy had been taken out of her comfort zone. But going to football games and other PR events gave her a social life she wouldn't otherwise have in between raising her fifteen year old sister, and for that she was grateful.

Champagne glass in hand, more for appearance sake because she needed to drive home and be sober, Macy looked around. She immediately caught sight of people heading towards them from the hallway. Damon, Evie and Jaxon Prescott, Bri's Major League Baseball player sibling, the word *player* having more than one connotation in his case, were laughing as they approached.

Jaxon's reputation for partying and sleeping around was legendary. Of all the Prescott brothers, Jaxon was the best looking, at least in Macy's mind. Clean cut, jet black hair, chiseled features, full lips she wouldn't mind kissing, and muscles galore, he'd tempt a saint.

But Macy didn't take Jaxon's occasional flirting seriously. She was his sister's friend and regardless he was a ladies' man in every sense of the word. Not that Macy had time for a relationship or even an affair, which put off most men. They didn't have patience with the responsibilities that came with being a parent to her sister. Not that Macy resented it. She loved her troublemaking sibling and had been Emma's primary caregiver even before their father died over six months ago.

As Damon, Evie and Jaxon stepped out of the

hallway, they nearly collided with Macy and Bri.

"Hi," Macy said, gripping her champagne glass to prevent it from spilling. It took all her willpower to keep from staring at Jaxon and she smiled at the three of them together, her gaze not lingering on any one person.

"Hi, ladies," Jaxon said, his gaze sliding over her, making Macy shiver. "You're looking good, Macy. White looks great with your tan. Hot."

She blinked, shocked he'd noticed the white halter dress she'd taken an hour to choose but she knew better than to take his words for more than they were. A throwaway compliment. Jaxon flirted with anything in a skirt. However she couldn't deny that his comment had give her a light, fluttering feeling in her stomach. "Thanks, Jaxon."

"So what were you three whispering about?" Bri finally asked.

"Just asking Jaxon what he's been doing," Damon said.

"You mean *who* he's been doing," Bri muttered.

Macy stifled a laugh and Jaxon narrowed his gaze at his sister. This was their usual dynamic, Bri calling him out, Jaxon getting not seriously annoyed but letting her know he didn't appreciate the jab.

"Come on, Macy. Let me introduce you to a few people from work. I think you'll like Adam Martsoff."

Bri ushered Macy away from her brother and she didn't mind. It couldn't hurt to meet a nice guy.

Unfortunately, she spent the next few minutes talking to a pleasant, if boring agent from Dare Nation, when her cell phone rang and she gratefully excused herself to take the call.

She saw her sister's name on the screen. "Hi, Em. What's up?"

"I'm bored at home. I want to go to the mall with Talia."

Macy sighed. "You're grounded, Em. You're lucky I didn't take away your laptop or phone. Then you'd really know what bored meant. Just sit tight."

"You're so unfair," Emma whined.

Macy rolled her eyes at the teenage dramatics. "Next time don't lie to me about where you are. I can't talk now. I'll be home in time for dinner. Bye." Disconnecting the call, she closed her eyes and groaned.

It wasn't easy raising a teenager alone and she really missed her dad, who'd been killed by a drunk driver on his way home from work. Although he hadn't been a very hands-on parent, there had at least been two of them against a willful teen.

At the sound of yelling from across the room, she opened her eyes to see Bri and Jaxon mid-argument. Concerned, Macy headed across the room, stopping short when family got there first.

"What's wrong?" Damon asked them.

"Ask Jaxon." Bri folded her arms across her chest, her glare one she used when in business mode.

A glance at Jaxon showed his face was flushed and Macy wondered what he'd done wrong.

"Let me talk to him," Damon said and Evie immediately headed over to Damon's mom, who stood with her gentleman friend.

"Come on, let's go have a talk," Damon said to his sibling but Bri shook her head.

"You're not leaving me out of this. I'm his publicist and he's damn well going to need one," she insisted.

"Why?" Damon asked.

Jaxon opened his mouth to explain, when Bri chimed in first. "You know that *chick he met at Allstars last night*?"

"Yes?" Damon asked sounding wary.

Bri held up her phone and turned the screen towards Damon. "Look what just hit social media? It turns out she's his general manager's daughter, home from college for a long weekend."

Oh my God, Macy thought. Jaxon had slept with his boss' daughter. He was a partier and a player but she knew as a star pitcher, he cared about his career. What had he been thinking?

"Dude!" Damon shook his head in disbelief.

"She was twenty-one and legal!" Jaxon tried to justify his actions.

"That won't make Brett Majors any happier with you," Austin said, coming up beside them. Grabbing Bri's cell, he watched the screen with a grimace. "Someone caught you two on a video grinding away while making out in the back hall of Allstars. And despite the fact that the owner demands discretion and privacy, the person leaked the video."

Macy winced, actually feeling sorry for Jaxon and how he'd had his privacy invaded. True, he hadn't been discreet but how awful must it be to have people watching your every move?

"And to say it has gone viral is an understatement. I'm getting notifications like crazy." Bri continued to shoot daggers at her bad boy brother.

"Dammit, Jax when are you going to get your shit together?" Austin asked.

"Come on guys. You never know where the paparazzi or fans are going to be," Damon said in an attempt to help his brother out.

"My point exactly!" Bri poked her finger at her brother.

"Not *my* point. I was saying cut him some slack." Damon tried again to stand up for Jaxon.

Austin groaned. "We are not doing this here. Not today. Today is Damon and Evie's celebration."

Always the head of the family, he took the lead and his siblings usually listened.

Glancing at Jaxon, he said, "I hope you're prepared for a meeting with ownership because once they see this video you're going to be in for it."

Everyone, including Macy, winced at Austin's furious tone.

After some more family discussion and murmuring quietly, Damon and Evie said their goodbyes, probably going home to enjoy their new found happiness, while Jaxon headed for the bar and asked for a drink.

Macy waited until Bri was alone and walked over to her friend. "Hey, are you okay?"

"If I kill my brother, will you bail me out of jail?" she asked, a wry smile on her face.

"If I can afford it, you know I will." Macy laughed. "Is he in that much trouble?"

Austin joined them. "He is."

"Because Jaxon is a manwhore," Bri said, grasping the drink out of Austin's hand and downing it all in one gulp.

"He needs to mature and settle down," Austin said.

"As if any sane woman would marry him," Bri muttered.

Macy chuckled. "Come on. I know you can't see him this way but he is easy on the eyes."

Bri made a gagging sound.

Macy kept an eye on Jaxon, who looked dejected, as everyone said their goodbyes. She wished she had some words of wisdom for him but Austin was right. He did need to pull himself together and act the part of a leader not a bad boy athlete.

A little while later, Macy left and headed home to her sister. She was twenty eight years old and a few years ago she'd lived in her own apartment. But when it became clear her father couldn't handle raising Emma alone, Macy had moved back into her childhood house, a patio home in a residential neighborhood just north of Miami.

As she approached, a bright red Mazda Miata Macy didn't recognize sat in the driveway, top down. If her sister had an older friend over, thinking Macy wouldn't find out, she'd be in even more trouble than she was already in.

Macy pulled around the other car, opened the garage, parked and exited her vehicle. Letting herself inside, she walked through the laundry room area and into the kitchen, stopping short when she saw who sat with Emma at the kitchen table. Bags of makeup and other items covered the surface with Sephora bags surrounding them.

Hell of a punishment. But the woman with Emma wouldn't know from discipline, structure, or anything else good for a young adult.

"Hi," Macy said, making her presence known.

"Macy, look! My mom's back!" Emma popped up from her chair, a smile the likes of which Macy had never seen on her sister's face and Macy's stomach twisted painfully.

Emma was a pretty girl who hadn't learned the concept of less is more when it came to makeup. She'd just started to wear it last year and after their dad died, she'd gone full out rebellious. But there were worse things than too much makeup on her face or the pink stripe in her hair. Macy actually liked the coloring if only Emma hadn't done it without asking permission, along with a second piercing in her ear. Anything she could do to defy Macy, Emma tried.

Ever since Lilah left when Emma was ten, she'd grown angrier over time and tried to get away with whatever she could on principle. The last thing Macy needed was her mother's return. Emma's mother had walked out on her daughter and husband five years ago, looking for someone with more money and who could give her a better lifestyle than Macy's father had been able to as an accountant. As far as Macy knew, other than an occasional happy birthday email, Emma hadn't heard from her mother since she'd left. Unless she'd been in communication with her and kept the information to herself.

"Lilah, this is a surprise," Macy said coolly, as she placed her keys in a basket on the counter.

"I've done a lot of soul searching and I decided it was time to come home to my baby." She reached across the table and squeezed Emma's hand, her long, manicured nails obviously freshly done. "And I arrived to find her by herself. Where were you, Macy?"

Oh she would not question Macy's abilities as a parent. She had no right. "Not that it's any of your business but I was at an engagement party and Emma is old enough to be home alone."

"Can mom stay with us?" Emma looked at Macy with wide hopeful eyes and Macy silently cursed Lilah, whose smug smirk told Macy she'd put her daughter up to asking the question.

Narrowing her gaze, Macy wondered what Lilah's agenda was because the woman always looked out for number one. "I don't think that's a good idea. We have a schedule and a routine and I'd like to keep things as they are."

She didn't want Emma to get used to having her mother around only for her to take off on her once again. The less time she was exposed to Lilah the better.

"It's okay, honey, I'll find a place to stay," Lilah sighed dramatically.

Ignoring the guilt Lilah tried to lay on, Macy

smiled. "Good. Now that that's settled—"

Emma pushed back her chair and rose to her feet. "You're such a—"

"Watch it," Macy said before Emma could finish her sentence. "Don't be rude to me. Now I think we should order dinner." Gritting her teeth, she turned to Lilah. "Would you like to stay?"

Shaking her head, her brunette hair highlighted with blonde swept beneath her cheeks. Lilah rose to her feet and gathered her Chanel tote, which must have cost three thousand dollars easy, and smiled. "I wish I could but I have a date." As she stepped around the table, Macy took in her obviously designer outfit and shoes.

So she was divorced. And home. Why?

"Come walk me out," Lilah said to Macy, her tone not boding well.

Macy waited for Emma to say goodbye to her mother, glare at Macy, and storm off to her room before turning to her ex-step-mother. "Okay cut the sweetness and light act. Why are you back? It can't be for Emma since you haven't bothered with her since you left."

Lilah straightened her shoulders, her attitude turning into the real bitch of a woman beneath the fake nice façade. "Because she's my daughter. When I left I knew your father would take good care of her when I couldn't—"

"Wouldn't," Macy corrected her.

Lilah pursed her lips. "Listen, she's my daughter. Her father died and I needed to wrap up a few things before I could come back for her but I'm here now."

Bullshit, Macy thought. "Nobody heard from you after dad passed away. You didn't even come to the funeral or extend condolences. I'm not buying this act. I don't know what your angle is but I know you have one."

"It's no act. I plan to take care of my girl."

"Good luck. I have custody. You signed it over to dad and I'm her legal guardian now that he's gone."

Lilah had started for the door then turned back to face Macy. "Something a court can easily overturn. It's not like you're doing a decent job parenting. I show up here to find Emma all alone. She told me she's grounded for no good reason, that you're strict and difficult. She's my child and I plan on getting custody." On that note, she walked out the door without looking back.

Macy's heart pounded inside her chest, fear and concern filling her at the thought of losing the sister she loved and the only family she had left. Macy's mother had died from ovarian cancer when Macy was six and it had just been her and her dad. True, he'd dated like crazy, hating the idea of being alone, but he'd loved his daughter.

Life had been good until the step mother from hell arrived when she'd turned thirteen. Her teenage years had been a nightmare with Lilah picking on her to be perfect but Macy had managed. And when Lilah disappeared, Macy was there for Emma.

She'd all but raised her sister and she had no intention of losing custody to a woman who didn't know how to be a parent.

*   *   *

Jaxon knew he'd screwed up but he resented being summoned by his siblings so they could reprimand him for his behavior in their positions as his agent and publicist. He was a grown man, dammit, and could fuck whoever he wanted. He acknowledged he'd made a huge mistake but getting reamed out wasn't on his list of fun things to do. He'd already been read the riot act by ownership of the Miami Eagles, the baseball team he pitched for, so suffice to say his mood was shit.

He walked into Dare Nation and headed straight for Austin's office, smiling at the main receptionist on his way to his brother's corner office. Quinn had a desk right outside.

"Hi, Jaxon," Quinn said, greeting Jaxon not with her usual happy smile, but a pitying grimace.

"I take it they're waiting for me?" he asked.

She nodded.

"How's my adorable niece?" Jaxon asked about the baby not only because he cared but the longer he avoided the firing squad inside that office, the better. His brother Austin had found baby Jenny on his doorstep, moved Quinn in to help him navigate being a dad, and the two had fallen in love.

Eyes lighting up at the topic, Quinn went on to tell him all the things the six month old baby was learning to do. "And she stands up and bounces on her chubby little legs and she's scooting backwards. Pretty soon she'll be crawling!"

"Said like a proud mama." Jaxon folded his arms across his chest and grinned. His brother was a lucky man—if Jaxon were to consider settling down with a wife and a baby lucky. Which he most certainly did not.

"Jaxon stop stalling and get your ass in here!" Austin bellowed from open door behind Quinn.

Quinn winced. "Guess you better move it."

"It's times like these when it sucks to have family as your agent and publicist."

Quinn's laughter followed him as he headed around her and through the door to face his siblings.

Austin stood behind his desk, arms folded, eyes narrowed, wearing a suit that demanded respect.

Beside him, leaning against the floor to ceiling dark mahogany bookshelf waited Bri. High heeled foot tapping, lips pursed and also dressed up in her finest suit, she met his gaze.

"Okay let's have it." Jaxon didn't mean to sound glib but realized based on his brother and sister's expressions, that's exactly how his statement had come out.

"Despite the fact that we discussed this at the party, let's start at the beginning since the damned video is everywhere. What the fuck were you thinking, Jaxon? Seriously?" Austin asked, his tone one of curtailed frustration and anger.

Jaxon curled his fingers into fists. "As I said, I picked up a girl at a bar—"

"The general manager's college-age daughter," Bri said.

"His twenty-one year old daughter," he repeated. "Not exactly a legal issue," he felt compelled to remind them. "Both of us were single, both adults, both—"

"Stupid enough to get video taped in the back hall, lips locked, your hand on her breast, going at it like teenagers. And the person managed to get your faces as well. Cell phones have other uses than texting!" Austin practically yelled. "You need to pay attention what's happening around you. And think smarter."

Jaxon rubbed his hands across his clean shaven face. "Again, we were both consenting adults." But the excuse sounded lame, even to him. He just found it hard to give in to Austin and just admit he'd screwed up.

Austin shook his head. "This isn't your first strike with management. There was the time you played still drunk—"

"I was just hungover and nearly pitched a no-hitter that day."

From the shake of Austin's head, that had been the wrong answer again.

"You fucked the general manager's daughter, Jaxon."

"I didn't know who she was!"

"That's the point! You should have known." Austin's voice rose again and his face flushed red.

Jaxon shoved his hands into his pockets so he didn't go after his brother like when they were kids. "So I'm supposed to do a background check on anyone I meet in a bar before I get laid?"

Austin closed his eyes and gritted his teeth before looking at Bri. "He's not getting it."

Bri shook her head. "Yes he is. He's just being stubborn." She walked over, grabbed Jaxon's arm and dragged him to the sofa on the far side of the room. "Sit down."

Being smart and not wanting to piss his sister off any further, Jaxon sat.

"Now you're going to pay attention to your agent. Not your brother, *your agent*, who has your best interest at heart. And as your sibling, you can be damn sure he's looking out for you even more. So shut up with the excuses and listen."

She was right, of course. Jaxon just didn't want to deal with the reality of what he'd done and the possible repercussions going forward for his career.

Leaning back against the sofa, he glanced at his brother and braced himself. "Go ahead."

Austin, having calmed down, walked over to the seat beside him and lowered himself onto the cushion, placing one arm on the back of the sofa. "As your brother, I understand who you are and why you act the way you do but dammit, you have to grow up. You're twenty-eight. Old enough to understand you're nearing the end of your pitching career."

Jaxon's heart squeezed in his chest. "Ouch."

His sibling was hitting on every insecurity he had about his past, old relationships, his job, his career, and his future. The things he partied and drank to avoid dwelling on.

He knew why he'd fallen into this lifestyle and it wasn't just the woman who'd walked out on him. Though Jaxon had been fifteen when his father died,

Jesse Prescott had been around long enough to have an impact. His asshole father had let him know in no uncertain terms if he didn't play football he was useless and no woman would want him. After losing Katie, Jaxon had gone about proving his deceased old man wrong by letting any cleat chaser available into his bed.

Austin didn't flinch. "It's my job to tell you the hard facts. I know you're in the off season but if you want to retire in disgrace you're well on your way because if the Eagles want you gone, no team is going to want to pay what's left on your contract and they're not going to trade for a twenty-eight year old with Tommy John surgery two years ago. The reality is you're too old for the partying and sex with groupie shit too."

"Linc said the same thing," Jaxon admitted, speaking of his best friend, his catcher, and a happily married family man who planned to retire at the end of next year when his contract expired.

Bri strode over and put a hand on his shoulder, offering sympathy where Austin appeared to have none. "I represent Linc too, as you know. He gives me no trouble, he goes to work, does his job and knows how to stay off ownership radar. Can't you be more like Linc?"

"You want me to get married and settle down but

that's not happening. No female wants to live the kind of life a baseball player does. I'm constantly on the road and play one hundred and sixty two games a year, excluding post season. Not to mention the fact that I was once in a relationship, came damn close to having that married life and learned it's not in the cards."

Katie, his college girlfriend, and the woman he thought he'd marry, had broken his heart, teaching him a hard lesson. His father had been right. No woman would want him and Jaxon refused to let that be true. So he'd locked up his emotions and lived life to have fun and prove dad wrong. Not even being dead eliminated the ghost of Jesse Prescott.

Austin groaned. "It is possible to live that life with the right woman. Look at Linc."

"You two sound like parrots," Jaxon muttered.

Ignoring him, Austin went on. "You won't be playing ball forever. You'll be more settled. And you don't want to be alone for the rest of your life."

"Says the man who not three months ago was a die-hard bachelor. Ever heard the expression the pot calling the kettle black?"

A muscle ticked in Austin's temple. "One, I didn't have to answer to anyone but myself and two, you might learn from my experience instead of being an asshole. Quinn is the best thing that ever happened to me. You should try dating a nice girl and not going for the ones who spreads their legs for anyone with a jersey."

"Eww." Bri shuddered. "This isn't a locker room."

"Well he needs to hear it," Austin muttered.

Jaxon frowned because no matter what his brother said, no matter how much of a valid point he might make, no way was Jaxon giving in. "Ownership can't make me get married," he muttered.

"No but they can order you to chill the fuck out or be suspended or worst case, cut. Is that what you want?"

Want even more Carly books?

CARLY'S BOOKLIST by Series – visit:
https://www.carlyphillips.com/CPBooklist

Sign up for Carly's Newsletter:
https://www.carlyphillips.com/CPNewsletter

Join Carly's Corner on Facebook:
https://www.carlyphillips.com/CarlysCorner

Carly on Facebook:
https://www.carlyphillips.com/CPFanpage

Carly on Instagram:
https://www.carlyphillips.com/CPInstagram

Carly's Booklist

The Dare Series

Dare to Love Series
Book 1: Dare to Love (Ian & Riley)
Book 2: Dare to Desire (Alex & Madison)
Book 3: Dare to Touch (Dylan & Olivia)
Book 4: Dare to Hold (Scott & Meg)
Book 5: Dare to Rock (Avery & Grey)
Book 6: Dare to Take (Tyler & Ella)
A Very Dare Christmas – Short Story (Ian & Riley)

** Sienna Dare gets together with Ethan Knight in **The Knight Brothers** (Dare Me Tonight).*

** Jason Dare gets together with Faith in the **Sexy Series** (More Than Sexy).*

Dare NY Series (NY Dare Cousins)
Book 1: Dare to Surrender (Gabe & Isabelle)
Book 2: Dare to Submit (Decklan & Amanda)
Book 3: Dare to Seduce (Max & Lucy)

The Knight Brothers
Book 1: Take Me Again (Sebastian & Ashley)
Book 2: Take Me Down (Parker & Emily)
Book 3: Dare Me Tonight (Ethan Knight & Sienna Dare)
Novella: Take The Bride (Sierra & Ryder)
Take Me Now – Short Story (Harper & Matt)

The Sexy Series
Book 1: More Than Sexy (Jason Dare & Faith)

Book 2: Twice As Sexy (Tanner & Scarlett)
Book 3: Better Than Sexy (Landon & Vivienne)
Novella: Sexy Love (Shane & Amber)

Dare Nation
Book 1: Dare to Resist (Austin & Quinn)
Book 2: Dare to Tempt (Damon & Evie)
Book 3: Dare to Play (Jaxon & Macy)
Book 4: Dare to Stay (Brandon & Willow)
Novella: Dare to Tease (Hudson & Brianne)

* Paul Dare's sperm donor kids

Kingston Family
Book 1: Just One Night (Linc Kingston & Jordan Greene)
Book 2: Just One Scandal (Chloe Kingston & Beck Daniels)
Book 3: Just One Chance (Xander Kingston & Sasha Keaton)
Book 4: Just One Spark (Dash Kingston & Cassidy Forrester)
Book 5: Just One Wish (Axel Forrester)
Book 6: Just One Dare (Aurora Kingston & Nick Dare)
Book 7: Just One Kiss
Book 8: Just One Taste

For the most recent Carly books, visit CARLY'S BOOKLIST page
www.carlyphillips.com/CPBooklist

Other Indie Series

Billionaire Bad Boys
Book 1: Going Down Easy
Book 2: Going Down Hard
Book 3: Going Down Fast
Book 4: Going In Deep
Going Down Again – Short Story

Hot Heroes Series
Book 1: Touch You Now
Book 2: Hold You Now
Book 3: Need You Now
Book 4: Want You Now

Bodyguard Bad Boys
Book 1: Rock Me
Book 2: Tempt Me
Novella: His To Protect

For the most recent Carly books, visit CARLY'S
BOOKLIST page
www.carlyphillips.com/CPBooklist

Carly's Originally Traditionally Published Books

Serendipity Series
Book 1: Serendipity
Book 2: Destiny
Book 3: Karma

Serendipity's Finest Series
Book 1: Perfect Fling
Book 2: Perfect Fit
Book 3: Perfect Together

Serendipity Novellas
Book 1: Fated
Book 2: Perfect Stranger

The Chandler Brothers
Book 1: The Bachelor
Book 2: The Playboy
Book 3: The Heartbreaker

Hot Zone
Book 1: Hot Stuff
Book 2: Hot Number
Book 3: Hot Item
Book 4: Hot Property

Costas Sisters
Book 1: Under the Boardwalk
Book 2: Summer of Love

Lucky Series
Book 1: Lucky Charm
Book 2: Lucky Break
Book 3: Lucky Streak

Bachelor Blogs
Book 1: Kiss Me if You Can
Book 2: Love Me If You Dare

Ty and Hunter
Book 1: Cross My Heart
Book 2: Sealed with a Kiss

Carly Classics (Unexpected Love)
Book 1: The Right Choice
Book 2: Perfect Partners
Book 3: Unexpected Chances
Book 4: Suddenly Love
Book 5: Worthy of Love

Carly Classics (The Simply Series)
Book 1: Simply Sinful
Book 2: Simply Scandalous
Book 3: Simply Sensual
Book 4: Body Heat
Book 5: Simply Sexy

For the most recent Carly books, visit CARLY'S
BOOKLIST page
www.carlyphillips.com/CPBooklist

Carly's Still Traditionally Published Books

Stand-Alone Books
Brazen
Secret Fantasy
Seduce Me
The Seduction
More Than Words Volume 7 – Compassion Can't
Wait
Naughty Under the Mistletoe
Grey's Anatomy 101 Essay
Grey's Anatomy 101 Essay

For the most recent Carly books, visit CARLY'S
BOOKLIST page
www.carlyphillips.com/CPBooklist

About the Author

NY Times, Wall Street Journal, and USA Today Bestseller, Carly Phillips is the queen of Alpha Heroes, at least according to The Harlequin Junkie Reviewer. Carly married her college sweetheart and lives in Purchase, NY along with her crazy dogs who are featured on her Facebook and Instagram pages. The author of over 75 romance novels, she has raised two incredible daughters and is now an empty nester. Carly's book, The Bachelor, was chosen by Kelly Ripa as her first romance club pick. Carly loves social media and interacting with her readers. Want to keep up with Carly? Sign up for her newsletter and receive TWO FREE books at www.carlyphillips.com.

Printed in the USA
CPSIA information can be obtained
at www.ICGtesting.com
LVHW052346251124
797634LV00034B/889